# Who Knows How We Are Made?

by Jerry M. Self

Cover art by Frederick Breedon

www.musiccityshooter.com

ISBN: 978-0-9962558-2-0

For Jay, Angela, Ashley, and Chancellor
I know the reasons

# Chapter 1: Arrival of the Deputies

The whoosh of the emergency room doors pulled the receptionist's eyes to the sheriff's deputies. Alex Smith, "Smitty," and Aleta Diaz sought a victim. The receptionist directed them down the hall where they could talk to attending Nurse Carroll. The nurse informed them that the victim causing her call to the police was undergoing surgery. She described his wounds and then asked them in turn what they had learned from the emergency medical tech.

"Not much," answered Smitty.

"A little more from the guy you told us called for the ambulance," added Officer Diaz. "We ran by the scene. The sheriff is out there now checking it out."

"Who's the runner?" asked Smitty.

"Don't know yet," said the nurse. "I'm going to recheck his clothing. But he had no ID on him at all."

"Not anyone from around here?" asked Diaz.

"I didn't recognize him. His face is badly swollen from a broken nose. A gash in his head had blood all over him. But even after I cleaned his face I couldn't be sure if I'd ever seen him before."

## Connie

Any parent would be proud to have a hero for a son. Until you consider the price attached. I hate to hear the phone ring any more. Although, I guess I didn't hear it ring when someone called to announce the end of all that warms and brightens my world. I still see Stephen, a slightly stooped, black form silhouetted against the blazing white lights of the den, the simple word, "Mom," abruptly halting the party. His brother, my first-born, in the emergency room. I feel Annie's hands on my back and arm. Twilight enters my soul; darkness follows not far behind, and with it, all dreams die.

My wonderful son, George, always full of surprises, challenged my dreams for him at every possible turning in his life. I'm sure he felt one step ahead of me, particularly when he announced to Arthur and me that he had signed up with the Navy recruiter in Austin. But I was proud of him then with the same tingly joy I felt when he bragged as a toddler about his "poo in the pot," or the hole-in-one he scored his junior year to help the Caliche Hills High School team win a tournament against their biggest San Antonio rivals, the Churchill Chargers. Everything he did for nineteen years, everything, they all fit my dream nicely even if stretching the seams of the dream. I would never say this to Arthur, of course, but I was even proud of George when he told his father that he would vote to re-elect President Clinton rather than go with the yard sign Art had stuck in our front lawn supporting Bob Dole.

## Chapter 2: The Party

Arthur and Connie had discussed a party to celebrate George's high school graduation. When George strode into the den with his coup d'état that college would be postponed and paid for by Uncle Sam, they just expanded the party to include all of George's major life changes.

So, Connie's dear friend Marie Alders, the sister she always wanted, and her daughter Annie helped her craft the party of the season for George. Not that Caliche Hills has a season, or a shopping center for that matter.

George, who loves his mother dearly but loves to tweak her sometimes, dashed through the decorating for his party, a gray blur in his sweats and out the front door throwing back, "I'll just run five miles. Clear the shower for me in about forty-five minutes." Connie was pleased to see him go. She knew he had plenty of time for a run, a shower, and to get into presentable clothes by party time. And he was out from under their feet. Good riddance, she thought, but then what does a mother know?

George wasn't gone ten minutes before Elspeth - George's girlfriend - danced in, eager to engineer some mocking surprise for George. She sailed through the front door in carnival mood.

"I've brought a present for Seaman Thompson," she announced.

"No presents," Connie said. "We told everyone, no presents."

"Oh, this won't upset your rule, Mrs. Thompson. Can I hide this in the hall closet?"

Connie said of course she could and chose not to ask questions about the silver wrapped and royal blue ribboned box.

She then grabbed Marie, anxious for some reassurance.

"I know I'm forgetting something," She told her.

"Nonsense, Connie. Everything is just perfect. All you need are the guests."

"And the guest of honor." Shaking her head, she looked at her watch, hoping George would not be longer than his allotted forty-five minutes.

"Let's walk through the house," said Annie. She is Connie's port in a storm. Of course Connie loves her guys but living in a house with three men who often behave as if they were three rampaging toddlers - well, a mother would need sweet, calm Annie.

Now Annie marshalled a parade through the house. Holding her mother's hand, she led Connie, Marie, and Elspeth into the den. A collage of Navy pictures - metallic hued ships and planes, sailors in white shaded with gray, all against teal seas and skies - placarded a theme in the middle of the room. A baby blue banner across the French doors to the backyard announced in a bold, red hand "Bon Voyage, Seaman Thompson!" From the den, they walked into the large kitchen, breakfast area. Yellow, red, green, and brown makings for tacos, chalupas, and burritos spread across the bar and the breakfast table. Three large coolers, appropriately navy blue, with various drinks on ice sat against a wall. In the dining room, the table was pushed against a wall and a Mexican food buffet awaited the guests. The dining chairs and some folding chairs lined the other walls. A brightly painted piñata and streamers added a festive touch.

Stephen, the youngest Thompson, and Arthur met the women in the entry hall. They had been setting out red stakes to indicate a parking area next to the driveway. Penelope, their Yorkshire terrier, trotted along after Stephen.

"Sylvester and Dan are here," said Stephen.

Marie took her cue to welcome her husband and son. The Alders, Dan and his parents Marie and Sylvester, usually called Syl, must have Italian blood in their veins, although they have never said so. Their dark coloring and slightly chunky bodies contrast so with the Thompson's slim blondness. When the two families converge, one could imagine a meeting of Scandinavian hunters and Mediterranean fishers. Elspeth captured Dan and Stephen, pulling them toward the closet. Probably she wanted to whisper secrets about her surprise for the "Seaman." Annie stuck with her mother.

Sylvester asked, "Where's George?"

"Out running," said Connie. "But he should be home any time." She turned to Art. "I really don't understand why he isn't already home. This just isn't like George."

"Oh, he found something he wanted to investigate." Arthur waved his hands in his calm-down-Connie gesture. "You know he sometimes gets distracted. Besides, it hasn't been that long."

"Okay. But I'm telling you, Art, if he's late to his own party, I'll wring his neck."

"Well the important thing," Sylvester said, "is when can we eat?"

"Not till other guests arrive," Marie answered. "But your question really was when can you eat. You don't care about our stomachs."

"Okay, I'll ask a more polite question. What can I do to help?"

Connie left that for Arthur to answer while - because she constantly rearranges things until the last minute - Marie, Annie and Connie toured the house one more time. They pushed the dining table to the end of the wall and then back to the center. Annie tugged on the banner. Marie hummed. Connie picked up everything in the kitchen, den, and dining room and set whatever it was back in the same place. The mantle clock startled her. "Is it ...?"

"Six o'clock," said Marie.

People began arriving. The noise level rose, as did the temperature inside. Connie made a point of moving people onto the back patio and asked Art to turn down the air conditioning. A couple of times she asked Annie or Stephen if their brother had returned. Quickly she lost count of how many people asked where the guest of honor was hiding. She was not happy. George had never pulled a stunt like this.

## Annie

George was in trouble with Mom. If he was blowing off the party we were giving him, he was in trouble with me. He and I are close, about as close as any brother and sister I know about, except for those occasions when I totally hate his guts.

When I was twelve our family did the beach thing at Mustang Island. That's the north part of Padre Island. I suppose going to South Padre means you're cool but we didn't know the difference. I love swimming and water skiing but hate fishing because everything to do with fish just reeks. Anyway, I thought it was going to be another summer like before. Stephen and I played Marco Polo, water tag, and water polo since I dunno when. Usually George was part of it but not always. If George played, we always had rules; otherwise, the game was a free-for-all. Of course, George's rules might be organized silliness, but still it was different from what Stephen and I would play without him. We started as toddlers swimming naked. By the end of the summer, we had the most awesome head-to-toe suntans. Mom loved finding bright colored suits for us to wear when we were old enough for that to matter. But we always had like sort of an unselfconsciousness together. At least Stephen and I were that way. Then we piled in the car for Mustang Island. We were between dogs at that time. In previous years, we took a pet with us or found a place for the dog to stay while we were gone. Mom and Dad took us to a cabin somewhere outside Corpus Christi. The boys wanted to hit the beach immediately but Dad insisted they help unload the car. He made a point of inspecting the car to make sure nothing had been left behind. The cabin smelled like mildew. Nobody else seemed to notice but I thought it was gross. The door opened on a living room with a TV that included a kitchen on the far end with like a breakfast table and four wire chairs. Two sofas smelled like sand and beer, a recliner and a beanbag chair completed the room. One of the sofas made into a bed - my bed. A bedroom on the left held a double bed - Mom and Dad's room. A bedroom on the right was for the boys with twin beds. A door next to Mom and Dad's room led to the only bathroom.

Stephen ran into the boy's room, dug his swim trunks out of his backpack, and stripped without shutting the door. George slammed the door for the sake of his privacy. I had not enjoyed the car ride from home and was feeling a little queasy. Mom asked if I wanted to go to the beach with the boys and I just nodded my head, found my suit and shut myself in the bathroom. The bathroom must have been clean because it reeked of disinfectant. I tried to open the window so some fresh air could breeze the room but I couldn't get the window to budge. I gave it a real hard push and then felt a warmth between my legs. For a split second, I thought I had wet my panties. Then I knew better. I just yelled. I didn't scream or anything, it was just a yell. The next thing I knew Mom was in the bathroom wanting to know what was wrong. I go, "I'm a woman!" I was sort of scared and proud and who knows what. The door was open and Dad just says, "Oh." He had this funny look on his face. Mom closed the door on him and began rummaging through her makeup bag. The first thing I said was, "I can't sleep out there." Mom stood up and looked at me and she goes, "You're sleeping with me. Your Dad will sleep on the couch." I was so glad because my chest had recently blossomed and Mom had bought me what she called a "training bra" and the first thing I thought when I saw that room was I'm not changing clothes out here. Okay, the second thing I thought after I thought this place stinks. So, she found a pad for me to wear and told me she thought swimming was out. I could wear my suit and just sun on the beach but no swimming. I tried the suit but it looked funny between my legs with that pad in there so I said no way, I'm not doing this.

When we came out of the bathroom, the guys were all gone: George, Stephen, and

Dad were on the beach. Mom and I talked all afternoon. She told me about when she got her period and stories about her friends. This was neat. Then the guys came back. George had a game made up involving a volleyball and the five of us in the surf. I said, "No way," and Mom said she didn't think the womenfolk were going to get into swimming suits. George went ballistic and he and I yelled at each other for five days. Then we went home. That was my greatest I-hate-his-guts scene in all history. He called me a spoilsport, a brat, a whiner, and I dunno what else.

One day after we were home for a while, he pulled me into the backyard and apologized. He said Mom had finally told him why we weren't swimming on our swimming holiday. He said he was sorry for being a jerk and that he understood about "growing pains." I didn't ask what he understood. I didn't say I forgave him. Actually, I didn't say anything. I just looked a sorta "So what" look until he walked away. Like, you know I enjoyed hating him for a week and wasn't ready to give it up. Anyway, after he walked off I knew I couldn't really hate him and besides having your older brother apologize is one of the neatest feelings in the world.

The next day we were hanging with some kids at a mall in Austin. Stephen and I were walking together and George was meandering along behind us. Some spazed out goofball ran into me and squeezed my breasts as he pushed off. George saw exactly what he had done and stuck his foot out as the kid ran past him. The dude landed flat on his face. "Sorry about that," George said. "Maybe you should watch where you're going." Then he said to Stephen and me "Anybody messes with one of us has to deal with the other two." Stephen didn't get what that was about.

## Chapter 3: The Phone Call

Stephen was so sure who was calling and so wrong. The party had moved outside on the patio allowing the ringing phone to make itself heard. George must have lost track of time and run further than he intended. Now he was calling to ask Stephen to come get him. Late for his own party! Not like George at all. Of course, it might be that George sprained an ankle and spent twenty minutes limping to the nearest phone. Either way their mother was already in a murderous mood. All this company here to celebrate George's nineteenth birthday, his high school graduation, and his enlistment in the Navy and he promised to be back in plenty of time before the party starts.

Stephen grabbed the kitchen phone and drawled, "Yes?"

Out on the patio, Coach Throckmorton told all who would listen a story about George hitting a bunker shot. Will McDonald smiled and nodded his head. His wife Florence's eyes glazed over leaving an expression signaling something like, "If I hear one more golf story ...." Annie touched her mother's elbow and asked who called. Connie told her she had not heard the phone ring. Just then, a soccer ball rolled across the patio followed by the next-door neighbor, Hans Bueller wearing a red fright wig and carrying a hockey stick. "Excuse me," he yelled. "May I play through?"

Hands at her cheeks, Connie cackled with laughter when Stephen stepped outside and called, "Mom!"

Something about his tone stopped everyone. In the thick silence he said, "George is in the emergency room at the hospital. We have to get there - now."

Of course, the guests had blocked in both the Thompsons' cars. Coach Throckmorton bundled the four of them into his SUV, one might see it as a mortician's hearse, and they left the neighborhood. As anyone could expect, Coach drove fast - people snapped heads around as if they were breaking a law, or at least the neighborhood code - but it felt to the riders like jogging through cold oatmeal. Connie asked Stephen what he heard on the phone. His blunt reply: we need to get there.

At the emergency room, an anxious Connie ran to the admitting window telling the girl there that she is George Thompson's mother. Where can she find him? "Wait there," she said and called someone. Long minutes later a small pale man in rumpled light green scrubs spotted with someone's blood lumbered through some double doors. He motioned toward an alcove where they grouped around him like hungry children waiting for a handout.

The doctor shook hands with Arthur. "Doctor Winchell," he said with a grimace.

"George is unconscious," he began. "He looks like he tried to tackle a half-ton pickup. A passerby called 911 and an ambulance brought him here about an hour and half ago."

"An hour and a half?" said Arthur.

"Yes, Mr. Thompson. Your son had no identification on him and it took quite a while for us to figure out who he was."

"Nobody recognized him?" The father sounded incredulous.

"I'm sorry about that," he replied. "When he got here he was unconscious and in critical condition. We have just finished an operation to repair an artery tear and are checking to see if we need to do further surgery."

"Surgery?" Connie cried.

"We are well prepared to take care of most emergencies." He managed a tight smile. "And we are not far from world class medical care in Austin, if we need it."

Connie grabbed Arthur's arm to keep upright.

"Will he, you know, be all right?" asked Annie.

"We're doing the best we can. It's early. I need to get back in there. Do you know where the waiting room is?"

Arthur nodded that he did and the man left them standing there. The four stood in place for a long moment. Lights flickered. Connie stared stunned. Stephen muttered something about it being incredible. Then Arthur took his wife's arm and they found their way through corridors until coming to the room reserved for families awaiting their loved one's fate.

"Why would someone hit George and just drive off?" Connie asked, speaking to no one in particular. "This isn't Houston or San

Antonio. I just don't understand. Did he mean George was hit by a truck or just looks that bad?"

"I think," Arthur spoke softly, "it was just an expression."

"Oh, Art. That makes it sound even worse."

Nobody responded. They sat. After a bit she asked, "Who was that man? I don't believe I know him."

"Dr. Winchell," said Arthur.

"You know him?"

"No. Never seen him before. I have heard about him. Harmon Klepner had gall bladder surgery here, remember? Winchell operated."

"If you've never seen him before, how do you know that was Dr. Winchell?"

"He told us his name when he walked up."

"I don't remember that. Probably it makes no difference in the world what his name is but I simply don't remember that."

Arthur asked the kids to get something to drink but Annie didn't want anything and refused to leave. Arthur said Stephen could go with him and they would be back in a minute. He stood to go but Stephen seemed reluctant to leave. After a moment, the son pulled himself to his feet. Before he left the room, he rubbed his mother's shoulder. "He'll be all right, Mom," he whispered.

## Connie

The room had no air. I couldn't breathe. Annie scooted next to me so I would put my arm around her. We hugged. She fidgeted and then stood. I noticed her party clothes, peach Capri pants with a gauzy beige top and straw wedges. She clashed with the drab, sterile box of a waiting room. She paced for a while and then sat opposite me. I stared at the door. Any minute Dr. Whoever will come in and tell us George has recovered and we can see him now. Well, maybe in thirty minutes.

The door did open and Willow Carroll floated in. Annie and I immediately perked up when we saw her. An early-twenties angel, Willow was the nurse who helped us survive my mother's illness and death. Mom had not actually been here in the hospital that much as we kept her at the house with the help of hospice. However, Willow had been so sweet to Mom while she was here and had called to check on her a few times during her last days at home. A petite brunette, her pink uniform set off her suntan. Connie prided herself on having played matchmaker between Willow and her husband, Lance Carroll, the young pastor of the Presbyterian church our family attended. Willow pulled a chair in front of the sofa where Annie and I sat and began an apology that it had taken so long to identify George.

"But I don't understand that, Willow. You know George."

"Yes, I do. And I was the first nurse to see him in the ER. His nose is broken and his face is puffy and was covered with blood. Even when we cleaned him up I didn't recognize him. Besides that, I was busy with his arm. The radius, a bone in his right forearm is broken. I concentrated on that while the ER doctor tended to his head."

"Is he going to - I mean, what kind of shape is he in?"

"Depends on how severe the head injury is, Connie. The arm and the internal injuries are less critical, we think. By the way, Dr.

Sauerwein was in the hospital and when we finally recognized we were treating a Thompson, someone called him in."

Hearing that helped some. Dr. Sauerwein has been our family physician since Art and I moved to Caliche Hills.

"Can we see him?"

"Later. Dr. Winchell has ... it'll be a little while, Connie." She smiled and patted on both of us then started to leave the room, our cage for the moment.

"We are supposed to be at a party right now."

"Oh," Willow said.

"This party is so out of character for our family because it was about and for George. You see, George plans all our special events. And cooks. Well, I do most of the pedestrian cooking. George, however, does appetizers, side dishes, and dessert. He bakes cakes, finds recipes for torts or tarts and streusels."

Willow smiled and looked over her shoulder.

"He often experiments and even invents desserts," I continued. "His cherries jubilee contains a flavor I have yet to decipher. If he sets a crusted something on the table, you never know what will be hiding beneath the top layer. Breakfast? You ask. Oh, George cooked breakfast for this family since he was ten years old."

"Mom," said Annie, "she didn't ask."

Willow gave a little wave and disappeared into the hallway.

Annie wanted to go find her Dad and Stephen. "If it's going to be some time, there's no sense sitting in this stupid place," she reasoned. She took my hand and pulled me into the hall.

Entering the snack bar area lifted my spirits some; the brightness invites your eyes outside the hospital. Windows all across two walls lighten the room. The crowd, if there had ever been one, had gone. Art wanted to know if we wanted a drink. He had joined us in the hall and guided us into the clinic's snack lounge. How many times have I been in this hospital because of our health issues or to visit others? Every turn in the halls challenged my growing disorientation.

# Chapter 4: In the Clinic Snack Lounge

Sylvester and Marie rushed into the lounge. Marie grabbed Connie and she let go a few tears. Guarding against a complete collapse, Connie allowed herself the comfort of leaning on a stalwart friend. Marie led her to a chair and they traded what little they knew.

The four Thompsons had simply run out of the house and jumped in the Coach's car. Sylvester and Marie shoved them out the door with the assurance they would close up the house and follow. Marie reported that the party guests had been full of questions, discussion, and suggestions. As Sylvester put it, "Most of it you don't need to know."

Arthur filled them in on what the doctor had said: George had been badly hurt, had lost some blood from an internal injury, and is unconscious from a couple of head injuries. He had a broken arm that is being set. He had gone through a surgery and now they were checking to see if they had missed anything.

"It sounds pretty serious," said Marie. "Have they given you any indication of, well, his recovery chances?"

"They tell us he's in good hands," Connie said.

Arthur quit his pacing and fell into a chair.

"What in the world happened?" asked Sylvester.

Arthur looked at Connie. She just looked so sad. Her face seemed to say what they both felt, that the world had suddenly turned upside down and made absolutely no sense at all.

"We don't know. It's just stupid. He was running. He had no wallet, only a cheap sports watch, and no car keys. He was on a five-mile run. You know he wasn't looking for trouble, wasn't looking for a fight."

Sylvester asked if the police had been by and Arthur told them Stephen was talking to them. Connie looked up as if she had just noticed that Stephen wasn't in the snack area. Annie touched her shoulder to remind her she still had her shadow.

# Connie

"Why are the police talking to Stephen? Shouldn't they be out discovering what happened?" I asked Sylvester but he was leaving the snack area heading who knows where. Art shook his head. "Who knows, Connie? Who knows what's going on here?"

I turned to Annie. "Did Stephen tell you anything more about what he learned on the phone?"

"Just we needed to get here."

"Art why don't you go tell them to do something useful. Why are they pestering Stephen?"

Art stood. "I think I will go see if I can find Stephen. Maybe they will have told him something that makes some sense."

I watched the back of his Aloha shirt leaving the room. Why were we in party clothes in a hospital?

Marie brought me a cup of coffee just the right shade of café au lait. It did help to be attended by friends. Annie chanted her mantra for me one more time; George is going to be fine.

"Of course he is, honey. Of course he is."

## Chapter 5: Nurse Watch

Willow Carroll watched Mr. Thompson walk toward the small office where she had situated the deputies. Shaking her head, she mentally retraced her efforts to identify George Thompson. She had helped patients with every sort of injury but never before had she not been able to recognize one. She wiped a hand across her brow and picked up the phone at the nurse's station desk. She almost gave up on the call when Lance answered.

"Honey, you need to get here as quick as you can. ... Well, because George Thompson is unconscious ... Yes, well, in a coma. ... I don't know. He was beaten. ... Can't you cancel? ... Yeah, well, really. You need to be here."

## Arthur

I guess my problem was I had only dealt with messengers. The cops, nurses, the doctor - all were messengers. I wanted to find those low-life scumbags who battered my son.

I did not yell at the cops. I just did not believe them. Stephen took the phone call from the hospital so the initial messenger was not even face-to-face. We did not get to see George at first. That made the doctor the first face-to-face messenger.

## Chapter 6: Deputy Interviews

The family all knew Smitty. He introduced Arthur to his fellow police officer, Aleta. She looked pretty much all business. Smitty explained to Arthur again, what Stephen had learned on the phone that without any means of identification on George it took a long time before anyone knew to call the Thompsons.

"Are you sure it's George?" Arthur asked and immediately realized it was a dumb question. He knew it was George and he hadn't been in to see him yet.

Smitty seemed to hesitate but then said, "Yeah. I've been in to see him and I know your son."

"Sure," he said. "It's George, then."

"Right, Arthur."

"Would you like to sit down?" asked Aleta. "We'd like to talk to you a little bit, Mr. Thompson."

They were in a conference room. Smitty and Aleta were now the messengers.

"Arthur, this appears to have been a hate crime."

"A hate crime! What are you talking about? What do you mean a hate crime?"

"There was graffiti on a fence," said Aleta.

"What did it say?"

"Well," she put a hand on his arm, "it wasn't finished. Maybe someone came along and scared them off. But graffiti usually indicates a hate crime."

"I don't understand. How could George be a victim of a hate crime? What is a hate crime? What are you talking about?"

Aleta started an answer but Smitty raised his hand.

"George have any, ah, enemies? I mean anybody give him a hard time about something?"

"No. People like George. You know, he's not the most social kid around. Not so much as Stephen or Annie, but people like George."

"Who does he see, what sort of people does he hang out with?" asked Aleta.

"What sort of people? Well, students, golfers, church people, two or three guys that are his buddies, his in-group, his girlfriend." He looked back and forth at the two officers trying to get a feel for what they wanted. "Not a lot of people."

"His girlfriend?" asked Smitty. "Who's she?"

"Elspeth. Just graduated with George."

"Elizabeth? Last name?" Aleta asked.

"No, Elspeth. Elspeth Reyes."

"Hispanic," said Smitty.

"Yeah."

"Who are his buddies?" Aleta asked.

"Dan." Arthur looked at Smitty and he nodded.

Sometimes Smitty, Sylvester, and Arthur played golf. Smitty had been a mainstay for the high school golf team in his day. Stephen would caddy for Smitty, Dan for Sylvester and George for his father. Arthur remembered one hot August morning. The men had meant to beat the heat with an early start and had failed grandly in that effort. Smitty had his competitors by several holes in match play and Stephen was talking up the prowess of his golfer, Deputy Smitty who was creaming two old men. Waiting for Sylvester to tee up on the par three fifteenth,

Smitty told Arthur that he had quite a pair of boys.

"Stephen has a keen sense of humor, Arthur. He's bright. And George really stands out whatever he's doing."

"Yeah?" Arthur looked at him, wondering what came next.

"Yeah. Look at him. We're all sweating buckets. Our clothes are soaked and we look like mops, very used mops. But George always looks like he just stepped out of the band box."

"... names?" Arthur heard Aleta say.

"Oh," he rubbed his eyes. "Ah, well, the golf team is about it. We go to church regularly but our three have been the high school department there. Actually there are a couple of other high schoolers and Stephen and Annie know them, but they're younger than George and he just ... I don't know."

"So," Smitty waved his hand, "how close are George and Elspeth? Don't think I ever saw him with a girl."

"Really good friends. You know, personally, I think that is a good thing. Get to be good friends before the romance part starts up."

"Right," said Smitty. Both of them began nodding their heads vigorously. "Right."

Smitty stood and suggested Arthur get back with his family. They would catch up with him later.

He found Connie, Annie, Marie, and Sylvester still in the snack bar with their drinks. Stephen was off with Dan it appeared. Arthur folded himself into a reversed chair in front of Connie taking both her hands.

"George was beaten up - deliberately," he told her.

She creased her forehead. Her husband was not making any sense at all.

"Art, how could that happen?"

"The reason the police are here is because George was attacked by someone, maybe a couple of people. He was beaten up."

"No, Art. Surely it was some kind of an accident." For the life of her, she could not imagine where he was getting this. Where did he think they were? Chicago?

He pushed himself closer and cupped her face in his hands.

"No accident," he said. "This was a crime."

Suddenly the numbness that had kept her in a fog wore off. She felt a stabbing in her heart and began to sob. Annie hugged her from the side and cried with her while Marie held her hand and pulled Connie's head against her.

"Sheriff's deputies?" asked Sylvester.

"Yeah. Smitty and a partner."

"You mind if I go stick my nose into it?"

"Knock yourself out. Don't see that it's anything but a waste of time, but be my guest."

Sylvester pressed his hand on Arthur's shoulder, told the women he would return and walked off.

After some time Sylvester came back to the lounge with Stephen and Dan in tow and informed Connie that the police wanted to ask her a few questions. Marie decided that she and Annie needed to go along, so the three gathered up purses and left. Arthur stared at them. How had Connie remembered to bring her purse along to the hospital in the first place?

# Arthur

I guess, now that I think about it, Sylvester
knows George about as well as any adult I
know. Because George and Dan spend a lot
of time together, they are likely to be with
one father as the other. Nevertheless, beyond
that, Syl is a passionate woodworker. He can
carve, tool, saw, chip, or plane any piece of
wood into something the wife just has to
have on a shelf somewhere. Marie's home
lacks nothing that can be supplied by crafted
woodwork. His avocation requires a massive
amount of patience and that patience makes
him a successful master craftsman who
trains young apprentice boys. Several
neighborhood youngsters had learned from
Sylvester. George is one of the more ardent
of his fledgling woodworkers. Or maybe I
should say he was - because with him off to
the Navy, his former life is past. George is
Syl's boy as much as mine, in a sense.
George and Elspeth. Elspeth is the lone
young woman who ventured into Sylvester's
garage in order to take up the chisel and
plane.

Sylvester told me George brought Elspeth
by one time to show her a Christmas gnome
he was carving for Connie's mantel. The

next thing anyone knew she had burrowed into their wood shavings and could not be extracted.

## Chapter 7: Not a Clue

Sylvester and the boys sat at the table with Arthur and then Stephen got up to go inspect the snack machine. Dan followed. Arthur looked up to discover he and Sylvester were alone.

"So you don't have a clue about what this means?" said Sylvester.

"It's the exact opposite of meaning. It makes no sense. The only clue I have is Smitty said he thought it was a hate crime."

"A hate crime?"

"That's what he said. I said something about George's girlfriend Elspeth Reyes and they sort of came to attention on that like it was a clue or something."

"What do you mean?"

"Oh, maybe that they might think someone didn't like the idea of a Gringo boy and a Mexacali Rose together."

"Hmm. Maybe so. But probably not."

"Oh really. So what's your opinion?"

Sylvester had no opinion for the moment. He grimaced and reminded Arthur that his son was a tough young man.

Yeah, George is one tough dude. But why would anyone want to hammer him into the ground? Why? Arthur banged the table again and walked to the window. The yelling came later after Sylvester resumed the conversation. The embarrassment followed after that.

After a while Connie, Annie, and Marie found the men staring into space.

At the snack machine Dan told Stephen there must a million things he would rather do than wait on an operation in a hospital.

## Stephen

When I saw the mantle clock signaling way past six, I thought something has happened to George. The phone ringing meant he was calling with some lame explanation that he had sprained his ankle and needed me to come drag his sorry butt home. Nurse Willow was the last voice I expected to hear. She told me straight up that George had been beaten. No way was I going to lead with that information. On the way to the hospital, I didn't know what else to do. I could not tell my folks what she had said on the phone. I know Mom just jumps to conclusions, fixes on either the best or the worst possible meaning, and runs with it.

I am just no help to anybody. Penny kept getting in my way while we scrambled to get out of the house. She didn't understand why she couldn't go with us. I can't talk to Annie. I want to but just can't. Right now, I seem to need to hang with Dan. We both, you know, just seethe. Is that a word? I think that's a word; maybe not the right word. We are boiling is what we're doing.

Actually, Dan's face blazed. I'm not sure how you do that but when Dan stomped up to me at the hospital, his fury burned off of his cheeks. "Do you know what this is about?" he hissed.

"I can guess."

"Cowards," he spat. "They caught him out on the Mason highway back behind the golf course."

"You know that's where?"

"Yeah. After I left your house I drove around where I thought he might have been jogging just to see what I could see and came across a police car still there."

We glared at the walls for a minute and then Dan asked what the doctors had reported. I told him we had not learned much since getting to the hospital. "Actually," I said, "the nurse told me on the phone as much as we have learned up to now. George is unconscious. They operated on him and that's about all we know." I looked at him. "Who do you suppose?"

Dan just shook his head. I pointed at the front door and we walked outside into a late hot summer evening. An older couple that I recognized from the church approached and asked about George. I told them we didn't know much and sent them inside to find my parents.

"It had to be someone who knew about George but not anyone that was close to the golf team or, I dunno ..." Dan muttered to himself for a moment. Then he pointed at me. "Football players!"

"Do ya think?"

"Yeah, I do. Some of them are macho jerks. They gravitate to lowest common denominator opinions, operate by herd instinct. They only know what the team captains tell them."

"Ah, I'm not so sure. But it sounds like you think it was guys from here."

"No. I don't. Not really. Whoever it was, spray-painted 'FAG' on a fence. Nobody from here would do that. I mean, they might think that but they wouldn't deface a Caliche Hills fence."

"So why did you say they were football players? I thought you were thinking guys on our team ..."

"No, I didn't mean that. I'm just trying to think what kind of person would do this."

"You saw the word?"

"Right. I did."

I shook my head. "I was afraid of that. Ever since those guys razzed me about my 'Older Sister' - by the way, they were cross-country runners."

"Who were they? Maybe they're the ones who did this."

"Naw, they're too chicken to even call George names. They were picking on his little brother."

"They probably don't know you lift weights."

We walked along the driveway that ran completely around the hospital. I thought back to the call from the hospital nurse and was glad that I had answered the phone. Willow Carroll works the afternoon/evening shift at the hospital as a trauma nurse. She said she had been attending George from the moment the ambulance delivered him and apparently, he was not recognizable. She checked his clothing a third time and discovered the name "Thompson" barely legible in the band of his old shorts. "His nose is broken and his face is badly swollen, Stephen." Well, my mother did not need to hear that. I just hung up the phone and ran to tell them we needed to get to the hospital. That George had had an accident. Once we got here, they found out that someone had beaten him. For the moment, Annie is sticking pretty close to Mom, which suits me because the moment I saw Dan headed our direction I knew I wanted to talk to him alone.

"It had to be several guys. George can handle himself," I said.

"I imagine so." He threw a rock. "I should have been running with him."

I looked at Dan. "I dunno. That might have just meant two of you in there."

"Still, we usually ran together."

I kicked a tire on an old pickup. "Fag, huh? Why do people do things like that?"

"Who knows? George stays by himself pretty much. Some people get ideas."

"Yeah, I know. But what I meant was - I mean, sure I can see how somebody might misunderstand George. But why do people pass judgment on other people, hurt people who disagree or live differently?" I swatted at a bee. "Or maybe aren't really different so much but just look different?"

"Oh George is different all right." We both laughed.

It was just George to be different. He always dressed just a little sharper than anyone else did. When someone expressed an opinion, either he had a clear contradiction for what had just been said or he agreed, but had a better reason for the opinion. This celebrate-George party was unique because George had not planned it or organized it. Okay, actually Annie and I do lots of work on family events meaning that I do the actual physical organizing - arranging a room or packing a van. George, however, mentally organized things. He told us what, when, and how. Then Annie and I put it in place. Mom would "ooh" and "aah" about George's genius. And I'm cool with that. It's just funny to me. George avoids attention anywhere else, but he gets a lot from Mom.

Dan asked me if I thought George had crossed somebody.

"George? When did George ever get crossways with someone?"

"I dunno," said Dan. "But you never know with some people. I just don't understand why somebody beat him up and then spray painted 'Fag' on a fence."

"Sounds like gangs or a school rivalry or something. Only that's San Antonio or Dallas, I guess. We never have anything like that around here."

"Yeah," agreed Dan. "And they would have painted a gang symbol or 'seniors rock.' Something stupid like that."

I looked at Dan for a long minute. "You know," I said, "I just don't get it."

Dan spit out an obscenity I didn't believe he would say.

"It's stupid," he said. "You don't beat somebody's brains out because you don't like his looks." I had to sit down. We had walked completely around the hospital and had come to a concrete bench out front.

## Chapter 8: The Women's Interview

It was Connie's turn for an interview. Marie and Annie insisted they should go with her. The women frowned at the small government looking baby-poop green office used by the admitting clerk. There were only three chairs in the office and barely enough room for the chairs and a small desk. A couple of gunmetal colored filing cabinets made it awkward if not impossible for five people to find places. Nevertheless, Marie and Annie refused to leave. Both stood, with Annie halfway out into the hall. Connie knew Smitty, one of the deputies, as a golfing buddy for her three guys. He introduced Aleta Diaz, his partner. Aleta's dark eyes and short black hair punctuated what Connie saw as a lot of personality. She immediately could see them as partners in more than just police work. In another setting, she would have asked Smitty if he were interested in dating Aleta. She had never been above matchmaking, especially when she was sure it would be beneficial for the young man.

"Mrs. Thompson, did George have any enemies that you know of?" Miss Diaz's face held such a caring expression. Nevertheless, Connie felt it was a stupid question.

"George? No."

"Had he gotten into a fight recently with anyone?"

"No. He hasn't had a fight since he was little boy."

"What about you, Annie?" Smitty took up the questioning. "Know of any enemies?"

"Uh, no," she bit her lip. "I've never heard him talk about anything like that."

They asked them more equally inane questions even including Marie in the process. Smitty assured George's mother they would find the responsible parties. She asked how something like this could happen in a small town. Both shrugged their shoulders. "Some thugs passing through," offered Smitty. They said thanks and sent them back to the others.

In the hallway, Annie said to her mother, "Dr. Sauerwein has put us back together every time one of us has been hurt. Don't worry, Mom, he's in with George now."

# Annie

Now, I know that some people have active imaginations. If someone knew us six or seven years ago, he might bring up that Halloween when George dressed up like a girl. Well, why not? At Halloween, you dress up like something you are not and try to fool people so they can't identify you. George pulled that one off for sure. Mom found him a sweater and a poodle skirt. She had an old wig and painted his face like Marilyn Monroe. Nobody knew who he was. They could look at the pirate and say "Hi, Stephen" or "Great Princess Leia, Annie," but no one made George. What's up with that? Here are three kids - two are brother and sister. How can you not know that the third kid is their older brother? Maybe they figured "she" was along with us as a baby-sitter or something.

## Chapter 9: An Escape

After some initial crying and hand-wringing Connie stood, declaring she had to do something. She strode out of the snack lounge with Marie and Annie following. She had no particular goal in mind but was determined to do something other than sit still. She stomped around a corner and immediately shrunk back into Marie.

"What?" Marie asked.

"Con and Mabel Whistleton," Connie said.

"Ohhhh," said Marie.

"Oh yeah, from church," said Annie.

"Right."

"Your mother would probably rather avoid them."

"Why? They're nice."

"They're boring and tedious," Connie answered.

"And they have no clue when they have overstayed their welcome," added Marie.

Marie peeked around the corner. She looked back at Connie, pointing back over her shoulder. "At the information desk," she whispered.

"Oh, nuts. Those volunteers are just too darn efficient and informative."

"They might help them find us," added Annie.

"Where does this hallway go I wonder?" said Marie.

Connie and Annie followed her.

Different doors had signs indicating important hospital activity centers: lab, x-ray, laundry, and stuff. They came to an exit and left the building, then found themselves behind the hospital among a couple of drab green dumpsters. The heat boiled off the asphalt. Connie started to open the door to go back into the hospital but Annie said not to because she could see the Whistletons at the end of the hall. So, they danced away almost attempting to fly to keep their feet off the drive. A lawn at the side of the building was nicely landscaped. Various shades of green under the shade of some oaks cooled their eyes if not so much their bodies. Connie pointed at Stephen and Dan in the parking lot.

"What are they up to?"

"Guy talk," suggested Marie.

Marie and Connie sat on a bench while Annie sprawled on the grass.

"Nice earrings," Marie said to Annie.

"I made them," she answered.

"Really! I love the beads. They match your blouse."

"Yeah, I really didn't like anything I had for this outfit, so I made them this morning."

"Aren't you the clever one?"

Connie chuckled, joining the conversation. "She's a genius. She suggested learning to make our own jewelry after Mom died. I think at heart she is some kind of recreational therapist."

"Does that mean you are selling jewelry-making kits at the shop?"

"Well, I already was. But not this. I sell some pretty pricey stuff. I think Annie gets her jewelry at a discount store."

Annie sat up and showed Marie her bracelet.

"Oh, matches the earrings."

"Of course, and it's built on form-memory wire. See, six strands wide, they open and then pop into place."

"Aren't you the belle of the ball!"

Annie stood and did a slow fashion twirl.

A new voice said, "What a lovely young lady."

The three women turned toward Mabel Whistleton at the front corner of the building.

Mabel and Con rushed forward as Marie and Connie weakly came to their feet.

"Your son said you were at the snack bar but we couldn't find you anywhere," began Mabel.

"Looked in the waiting lounge," added Con.

"All up and down the halls," said Mabel.

"Thought I saw you going out back," Con waved.

"Gave up and were leaving."

"I said isn't that Art and Connie's daughter?"

Connie braced herself and said, "How nice of you to come."

"Oh, Connie, I'm so sorry to hear about your boy. Is he going to be all right?"

Managing a weak smile Connie said, "We think so. A little patching and a cast on his arm and he'll be good as new."

"You know, Con's second cousin in Florida was beat up by a gang." She turned to Con for agreement. This could be a long story.

Annie took her mother's arm. "Mom, look at the time. The doctor wants to meet with us now."

"Right," said Marie yanking on Connie's other arm. "Thanks for coming by, Mister and Missus Whistleton." The three marched off to the front door.

Entering the cool air of the vestibule Annie asked, "Mom, should you make a list of acceptable visitors? Stephen didn't know he wasn't s'posed to direct them to you."

"No, honey, no one is off-limits. Con and Mabel are well-meaning people. She brought a casserole to the house when Mama Teresa died. Remember? They're good people. It's just - well, I feel as if I am giving up part of my soul listening to them tell their stories. That may be fine some other time. Not right now."

"You know something, Annie," said Marie, "a social life for some people amounts to visiting with people in hospitals and funeral homes."

"Yuck!" said Annie.

## Stephen

I guess I've known for a long time that some guys looked at George as though he were a little too much his mother's boy. But I've always known his personal toughness and discipline. It's one thing to realize your brother is neater and pickier than you are. It's something else entirely to think that this means he's homosexual. I don't know, having never given it much thought, I guess there's nothing wrong with being gay. Or, maybe there is. I can't remember ever hearing my family talk about it. I'm not sure anyone in Caliche Hills is homosexual. Well, there are a couple of people in town - maybe. I have never known of or about a gay teenager. Would you know you were homosexual if you were a teenager? Maybe.

I looked at Dan. "Do homosexuals play golf and do woodworking stuff?"

"How would I know? I've never known a queer."

"I don't think they like being called that."

"Yeah, probably not. But, again, how would I know?"

"Dan, did you ever think George was gay?"

"No! No, absolutely not."

"You never thought he was a little too neat, a little too prim, a little too fussy?"

"Oh yeah. All the time. That's beside the point."

"What about this 'manhood' thing with the Navy?"

Dan rubbed his head. "Yeah, what was that about?"

We both looked for a response somewhere in the grass behind the bench.

"He said," Dan began and then hesitated. "He said he wanted to be sure he was a man before he got into any serious study about what sort of man he was going to be."

"Yeah. I told him it wasn't that hard to decide on a major."

"But you know he isn't going to college for fun and games."

"I guess not since he turned down a golf scholarship at TSU."

"I thought he was disappointed it wasn't UT Austin."

I shook my head. "Nah. He told me it was time to grow up."

"You can grow up in college and at a more comfortable pace than joining the Navy."

"What about Elspeth and girls? I don't remember him ever having a real date."

"So? I haven't had that many dates. We're, well, we're just not lovers. I mean I know several guys who are clumsy with girls, bashful and stuff. That doesn't make us homosexual. I'll tell you this, Stephen, I'm really, uh, well, scared of girls, to be honest with you. But I'm really sure that I'm a straight hetero. I don't have any doubt about that."

"And you'd say the same about George?"

Dan rubbed his chin and looked across the parking lot.

"Dan?"

While Dan spaced out, my mind raced other places. I thought about Wendy Sturgis. That girl would easily win a Miss Teenager contest. She just would. I told George I wanted to ask Wendy for a date and he said go for it.

"What do I say?" I asked.

"Just ask her to go out with you. What kind of date?"

"A movie, I guess. The new Star Wars film is out."

"So ask her to go to a movie with you."

"Should I ask her at school or call her? I better call her. Just me and her on the phone. At school somebody might butt in."

"Right. Call her. How about right now? This would be a good time."

"Not right now. Right now? I don't think right now."

"Why not?"

"What if she's not home?"

"Tell her mother you'll call back later."

"That's not good. If I call, I want her to be there."

"It doesn't have to be perfect. Chances are she's home right now. Call."

"I've got an idea. Let's double date. You call Elspeth and then I'll call Wendy and ask her to go with us. That would be easier."

"Well, no. It wouldn't be - how would it be easier?"

"It just would. Call Elspeth and then I'll call Wendy."

"Elspeth wouldn't go if we called it a date."

"Really? Why not?"

"She's just turned off by the whole idea of dating."

"You two have gone on dates before."

"No, not really. We have gone some places together with other people but it was a group thing. We've never had a 'date'."

"Call somebody else then. I need you to go with me. It'll be a lot easier to ask Wendy to go on a double date. Call some other girl."

"What other girl? I don't know any girls. You're the one interested in girls. I'm not."

"What do you mean you're not interested in girls?"

Little creases formed at the edge of George's mouth. "I'm working on my golf game," he said.

One time we were walking down the hall at school and Samantha Hanson ran up to George and kissed him on the cheek. He looked surprised and she laughed and said, "What do you think of that, Georgie?"

"Did someone pay you to do that?" he asked.

"Someone dared me to do that." She stood fists on her hips with a big grin on her face. "Now, kiss me back!"

George laughed. "No one dared me to do anything."

"I dare you," she said.

"Too late. It's time for class."

As we walked away from her, she laughed and called after us. "I guess it's true then."

George did not say anything and I did not ask.

Dan interrupted my jog through my memory with a complaint about the heat.

"Yeah," I said, "You know what? We oughta head back inside and see what's happening."

## Chapter 10: Inside Again

Once again, Annie led the parade as the women reentered the building. The air conditioning refreshed them and for a moment, they all smiled. "Heard anything?" Stephen's voice behind them yanked the women back to reality.

### Annie

This day started with some laughter. George insisted on preparing breakfast since the rest of us were going to be putting together his graduation/Navy enlistment party. He does that occasionally. He can do scrambled eggs, hash brown potatoes, omelets, French toast, waffles, or pancakes. Come to think of it, so can Stephen, so can I. We just don't unless Mom or Dad tells us we need to for some reason. Probably almost anyone could fix one of those breakfast dishes. The difference is that George volunteers and enjoys it. What's up with that?

Anyway, no one objected. I mean, why would we? He baked pancakes. Now who does that? A couple of times I have done pancakes on a griddle, and that's what George usually does, but this time he baked them. And they turned out pretty good except for the surprises. Stephen and I got pancakes with chocolate chips. Phat! I'm not very sure about Stephen but I liked them - a lot. For Mom and Dad the pancakes had raisins in them. I guess they saw what we had and maybe sort of had their mouths ready for chocolate chips. Raisins baked in pancakes? Well, I don't know because I didn't taste them. Mom and Dad were surprised. Mom wondered which kind George was eating and he said he had cherry jam in his. Then Dad stood up and cut pieces out of different pancakes and distributed different bites to our plates. George acted out a mock horror at what he was doing. Stephen thought it was pretty funny and we all laughed about it. Although I didn't think it was that funny and didn't even taste the other pancakes. But that was okay.

We bounced through the day in party mode. George took his putter over to Dan's house. A couple of summers ago Dan, George and Stephen created a putting green in Dan's back yard. Stephen did most of the planning and a lot of bossing on the project. He's the green thumb guy. That is about the only way he could ever get away with giving George and Dan orders. They put up with it, though, because all three of them wanted that putting green. And it turned out great. I mean, what do I know about putting? Okay, it has several holes, they call them cups, and a lot of undulations. Unnh, the way they say "undulations." "Isn't your green awfully bumpy?" "No, it's s'posed to be that way. Those are undulations." Give me a break. Anyway, he was off doing his golf thing. Dad and Stephen ran errands getting last minute stuff. Mom had me vacuuming while she dusted. I think we just did this already. Anyway, that's what we did and we made sure not one thing in the house was out of place or dusty or broken or whatever.

Marie came over after lunch and we moved into high gear decorating at warp speed. Marie kind of grows on you. Mom and I are maybe a little bit hyper. I mean, not ADHD or anything, but we talk a lot and fix things and keep moving. Marie is more quiet and calm. You might say she's "laid-back," but I wouldn't say that because to me, laid-back means you're not quite there. You know what I mean? It means, to some extent, you have checked out, not paying attention, don't really care. I suppose not everyone means that when they say "laid-back" but that's not how I would describe Marie. Mom had some artsy ideas about George's senior year and his Navy enlistment for display in the den. Marie had suggestions about how to mount and glue all that stuff together so people could see it and it would stay in place all afternoon and evening.

## Chapter 11: Back to the Waiting

At some point, everyone settled in various corners of the snack lounge staring into space. Elspeth found them there. She ran up to Connie, eyes wide, eyebrows arched; her face asked the question she could not voice.

"We don't know anything," Connie told her. She stood to hug Elspeth and tell her about the surgery. Something in her young, distraught face caused a catch in Connie's throat. Arthur stepped up and threw an arm around her shoulders. Then he let his wife burrow into his arms and they held each other for a moment. Connie wondered if they shouldn't go back to the waiting room in case someone came looking for them with word on George. Arthur told the group what they were doing and then George's parents started back up the hall. Elspeth joined Dan and Stephen in their corner. Connie asked if Arthur learned anything from Smitty and Aleta. "No," he said, "They just wanted to learn as much as they could. They weren't talking."

"Learn what? We don't know what happened." She took his chin in her hand. "What did happen, Art? What did happen?"

"I have no idea, hon. None."


## Connie

The waiting room was vacant and felt like compressed desperation. Cushioned western motif furniture invited restless pseudo-lounging while something precious was being sliced, reattached or sewn together down the hallway and around an antiseptic corner. We needed to be here to receive the word. But I felt the breath squeezed out of my chest every time we entered the room. Annie squeezed my hand and sat beside me. Yes, that's right. She had tagged along.

For some reason Art decided to talk about George and Elspeth. He started by asking Annie why George had not taken Elspeth to the prom.

"She wasn't interested, Dad. George would have been glad to take her if that's what she wanted to do."

"Well, why not? They went on other dates didn't they?"

"Not really. They went places together or sometimes Dan and the two of them did. But they were just hanging together. It was never a date."

"Are you saying ...?"

I leaned over and touched his arm. "Art, Elspeth just isn't that interested in dating guys."

"Elspeth isn't?"

"No, and George and Dan are comfortable with that. So, Elspeth is comfortable with them."

"Okay," he shrugged. "But, well, that's fine. But you're not saying that Elspeth is a lesbian?" Crude question. I pursed my lips and looked out the waiting room window.

"Are you?" he asked.

"Elspeth hasn't told me that."

"What has she told you?"

"Very little, actually. George told me - well, one time I said something to George about asking Elspeth for a date - no, that wasn't it. They had gone to that Lord of the Rings movie and I asked him how his date had gone. He told me about the movie and what Elspeth had said about it and what he thought and then he said it was not a date. He explained that they were just friends. You know Art; they've known each other a long time."

"Yeah, I know that. What's that got to do with it?"

"Right. I said almost the same thing. Friendship is great, I told George, but you can still date your friends. And he said, 'Mom, you just don't understand.' Now Annie, why do you kids always pepper your conversations with that phrase?"

"Because it's true?" Annie raised both palms.

"Sure," Art said, "like your mother was never a teen herself."

"Anyway," I continued, "he told me Elspeth really wasn't interested in boys. She had tried to talk to some girls about it and they pretty well ostracized her."

"That's right, Mom. She doesn't really have any friends at school."

"Yeah, and then sometime later she made a point of telling me that George had told her about our conversation and she wanted to know what I thought about it."

"What did you tell her?" Art asked.

"Oh, just that it's a confusing world and, I don't remember exactly, something about she was always welcome at our house."

"And that was it?"

"No, she had a question for me. She wanted to know why couldn't a woman just live her own life and that be good enough. Why does a woman have to get status or importance from a man?"

"And you told her your husband and sons got their status and importance from you."

"Actually that is precisely what I told her."

Annie leaned toward me. "That doesn't mean - she didn't say she was gay."

"No, Annie. Not at all."

Art snorted, "Things are bad enough without us having to ferret out the homosexuals in our community."

"If we find out a friend is gay," Annie hesitated, "don't we have to just, like live with it?"

"Let's not follow this line of thought," I objected. My words seem to disappear in the furniture. The air conditioner hissed at us.

"Okay," Art reemerged. "Elspeth needs a friend and George is a good choice. I would have to say I am proud of him like I am always proud of what our three kids do. He could still be her good friend and date some other nice girl. Why isn't he dating someone else?"

"Like who for instance?" asked Annie.

"Art, George is unconscious in ICU right now," I glared. "Why do you care about his girlfriends or lack of them?"

"Because, that may be the very reason why he was beaten to a pulp. Somebody thinks our son is a queer and they chose to bash the gay."

My jaw dropped.

Before I had a chance to respond, the doctors walked in.

## Chapter 12: Medical Update

Doctor Winchell was a small man and he looked stooped and tired. He smiled weakly at the Thompsons and told them George appeared to be stable but still unconscious. He had checked in detail all of George's vital signs. The worst injuries seemed to be a broken arm and a concussion. The next few hours would probably lead to recovery or an indication of further treatment needed. No one could see him now but, perhaps, in a couple of hours there could be quick visits. Doctor Sauerwein towered over the other physician. He encouraged his friends that recovery was now between George and God. All anyone could do right now was wait. If they were so inclined, as he knew they were, this would be a good time for prayer.

Arthur raised his hands. "You don't sound terrifically confident."

Dr. Winchell shrugged. "Well, I won't be confident until George walks out of here on his own steam. However, let me assure you of two things. We are doing the best we can for your son and if he needs more and better treatment than we can give him, he will be immediately transported to Austin." After another tight smile, he turned and left the room. Sauerwein gave Connie a quick hug, patted Arthur's shoulder and followed Winchell's path.

As the doctors left, Sylvester, Marie, Dan, Stephen, and Elspeth came in. Arthur repeated what the doctors had said. Marie wanted to know when anyone could see George.

"They didn't say anything about that," Connie said.

Arthur looked at her with a puzzled expression and then said, "Dr. Winchell said maybe in about two hours."

"Art, are you making things up?"

"Maybe you were listening to Doc Sauerwein and missed it hon."


### Arthur

I remember we spent some time in that postage stamp of a waiting room. Elspeth floated in and out. Syl, Marie, and Dan were with us and then somewhere else. At some point, I thought Connie, Annie, and I had a little family privacy so I asked Annie if she thought her brother was gay. Well, I asked what his relationship with Elspeth was like, and then I asked what she thought. Both of them got very defensive. "Your son's a good boy!" and "Dad you can't say things like that about George!" Man alive! "How can you talk like that while your son is in the next room unconscious?"

So, I told her, "He may be there because someone thinks he's a homo!"

Why on earth did I dump that on her? She was just regaining some personal strength after her mother's death and now someone attacks George. I sure did not need to add to it.

Fortunately, Sauerwein and Winchell walked in and interrupted my stupid speech.

They did not have good news. George had come through the surgery but barely.

## Chapter 13: An Apology

Arthur stood in the doorway, his back to the retreating doctors. Annie finished a long hug for her mother and then moved to deliver the same comfort to her father.

"I'm sorry girls," he whispered into her hair. Releasing his daughter, he took Connie's hand. "I really am frustrated, angry, and confused. But I didn't mean to take it out on you guys."

"We're hurting, too, Dad," said Annie.

Connie nodded at her daughter, tears streaming down her cheeks.

### Connie

Isn't it funny how your children can be so much alike and yet so different? For instance, Stephen arranged all his toys either according to size or according to weight. Annie never arranged anything. All her toys or clothes would appear to be in jumbles or piles. Yet they would be organized in some sort of color coordination scheme. On the other hand, George - everything in his room had a place. Color, size, weight, age, functionality, durability - everything had a place and every place was relative. You might ask him (we rarely did) why is this here and not there? First, he would give you that "Isn't it obvious" glare and then he would explain, "I'm not going to need this unless I am through with that and then I'll want to be able to find the other." Or, something like that.

And so when it came to family events George just naturally had the details in his head before the rest of us realized it was birthday or anniversary time. It was always different but appropriate. He had us in stitches with a dumb-emails theme for Arthur (computers are his work and his hobby, primary hobby, that is, before golf). Somewhere he came up with a smelling game for Annie's birthday. Even blindfolded she recognized every odor he waved under her nose. The rest of us could not guess three out of ten. For Stephen's birthday one year he directed a family outing to a wildflower farm near Johnson City. Hours after we got there Stephen wasn't ready to leave. For my birthday last year, he took me on a scavenger hunt ending at my shop where my current student employees and several former ones returned from college presented me with small portraits each one had done of my family members, our home, and the shop. The paintings decorate our bedroom walls and the hall in the bedroom wing of our house. Recently he told me he had an idea for our twenty-fifth anniversary and that is three years off.

I am constantly amazed at the creativity he can engineer in this small town. I suppose it's a weakness of mine, but I sometimes feel the lack of major shopping centers limits one's ability to be clever. Now why would an artist like myself feel that way? Caliche Hills, our small village in the Texas Hill country settled next to San Marcos, serves Austin as a bedroom community. Many of us have husbands like Art who drive daily to Dell Computers or a government office in the big city; although a good many are retirees from petroleum companies in Houston. They live in the big homes hidden by live oak trees set off the road where one would never suspect a house existed. Our graduation-birthday-naval enlistment party would not have measured up to their standards, I suppose, but it promised to be about as big an affair as our modest two-story rambling home would hold.

George was the focus of the party, as he was the center of almost anything I have done for the last nineteen years.

Oh, but Annie, my second skin, my shadow appendage, now she is my dream-daughter. The heart of our mother-daughter tandem flourished with my mother's illness and death. Eighteen months ago, I drove into San Antonio to ferry Mom to a routine doctor's visit. Annie went along, making for a pleasant outing - a girl's day out while Art and the boys were off to a golf tournament in Fredericksburg. Decked out in my aquamarine slacks and Annie in plum denim shorts we chattered our way down highway 281 for an hour. Annie loved her grandmother, her Mama Teresa, dearly, not the least because she was the only granddaughter and therefore Mom's most favorite person in the world. Mom greeted us cheerfully although she was coughing a good bit and I thought somewhat lethargic for my "good to go" mother. I am sure someone else could have driven her to the doctor. However, I was a terrier about

Mom's health. After her eyesight dimmed to the extent of losing her driver's license, I had done the entire serious errand driving for Mom.

Mom's doctor showed a great deal of sensitivity to his patients. Mom insisted on seeing the doctor by herself. She asserted her independence, more so as her need to depend increased. The doctor, bless his heart, always took a little time, after her visit, to bring me in on her medical condition. There was always something: blood pressure, hormones, calcium deficiency, cataracts, you name it. Yet those are expected bills you receive, part of the price of living a full life. Mom's doctor could be upbeat in telling me of needed life course changes, or how to meld a new prescription into her daily procedure. With this office call, however, he sent a nurse to invite me into the conference with Mom and her doctor. Annie asked me what that meant. I didn't reply, just waved a "hold it for a minute gesture" and followed the nurse.

He did not like what he had found and wanted to run some tests on Mom. Within a week, we found what I had feared when first walking into that conference. She had cancer. Mom met the news matter-of-factly. The usual "putting your affairs in order" meant that she had letters to write, people to call, friends to see or invite over. She already had a will, had signed over a durable power-of-attorney to me, and a living will in the doctor's file.

There was an operation. Cervical cancer. They just sewed her back up. They said chemo, radiation. She said no way.

She moved in with us.

"Mother we need to play a duet," Annie announced to me one afternoon. We had Mom in a hospital bed in our den for the last rush to darkness. What I call a den, Art calls our Great Room. Indeed, the room is large, with a fireplace, dusty rose textured walls, French doors leading to a patio, comfortable overstuffed desert sand furniture on a burgundy carpet, a console TV, and a spinet piano against one wall. With Mom's bed taking up the middle of the room, spaciousness gave way to a feeling of living in a large-scale sardine can. In spite of our best efforts, Annie complained that the room smelled like a nursing home.

Penelope nudged legs until someone would lift her onto the bed with Mama Teresa.

They shared many a quiet conversation. Occasionally Penny would tongue-wash her face. Mom called her the "Love Puppy." Most of the time the two of them napped together.

"The piano's in there with Mama Teresa," I noted. I was sure that was explanation enough for why we had given up the instrument for over a week.

"That's one reason we need to play. Mama Teresa would enjoy hearing it."

"I don't think so, hon. Besides, I just can't."

"That's another reason." She turned me and pushed until we seated ourselves on the bench.

"Mama Teresa," she said, "here's something for you." There was music in front of us and Annie began to play. She sat on my right playing the upper registers. I did as I was told. What we played escaped me immediately. It was only one piece. After that, Annie choreographed a duet every day. I suppose the music brightened Mom's days. I believe it helped me survive as well.

The cancer leaked into every organ quickly. Hospice played the role of angels in her life for about six weeks and then she died. She died as she had lived, masterfully. Annie and I stumbled and bumbled through it. Or, maybe that only described me. Annie simply followed me through my malaise.

Mother may have been ready to go but I was not ready to let her go. While living through that bleak nightmare I could not focus on the blunt, cruel fact that Mom was gone. I still find it hard to believe that Annie and I can't jump in the car and within an hour be shopping with Mom between us. Grieving sapped my energy, leaving very little of me for Art or the boys. Annie became an afterthought. She was my second skin: never noticed, never absent. Only later could I remember that she was never not with me.

My days dribbled along, dark gray packing foam seemed to fill the rooms. I burned a supper for the family, forgot to fix myself lunch and served green beans, lima beans, and English peas for supper one evening.

One night I could not sleep so finally I got up and stumbled into the kitchen intending to heat some water for hot chocolate. Standing in front of the sink, filling the teapot with water, it occurred to me that this was Mom's perennial answer to sleeplessness: hot milk, sometimes chocolate but not always. When I turned around, I saw a dim figure in a gown of some sort standing in the doorway. I had turned on a light over the sink but it did very little to shed light throughout the room. At first, I thought it was Annie so I said, "Can't sleep either?" Then I realized she was a little smaller than my daughter and slightly stooped. "Mom?" I whispered. I thought I detected a smile, and then the figure faded. I rubbed my eyes and took a few hesitant steps toward the door. The next morning for breakfast, I couldn't find my teapot to make tea for Art. He asked what had me in a dither and I told him the teapot was missing.

"Here it is in the sink," he pointed.

"Oh, yeah," I said.

"Whatta ya mean, 'Oh, yeah'?"

"Nothing," I said. "I just forgot where I put it."

Sometime later, days I think, I told Art I had seen Mom. He didn't say anything. Gave me a hug. Kissed my head. Finally, he said, "She loved you, you know."

Mostly I just sat. For long periods, I would just sit and stare. Not stare at something, or out of the window, or at a book, a magazine, or the television. I just stared. Occasionally Art might ask me what I was looking at and I had no idea.

Of course, people die. I know that. Everybody dies sooner or later. Someday, even I will finish my days here on earth. I do not know why Mom's death hit me so hard. It just did. Dad's death a few years ago had not been so devastating. Marie told me I needed to talk to someone. She suggested a woman she knew personally who did therapy in South Austin. I was sure I did not need anything that clinical. "What about our pastor?" She asked. I didn't want to trouble him. "How about lunch then?" That seemed a complete change of subject and a better idea.

Lunch turned out to be a gathering of four women. Bethany from Kyle, Jane from Blanco, Marie and I - we arranged ourselves around a rustic table in a small Hill Country restaurant near Fredericksburg. Bethany's husband, I quickly discovered, died of pancreatic cancer two years earlier. Jane's parents drove into a low water crossing and drowned when their car was swept away. Marie reminded me she, too, was a double orphan. I told her I was not familiar with the term.

"It means you've lost both parents."

"Sure. I understand. I just hadn't heard the expression before."

Turns out all four of us were double orphans.

"Isn't that redundant?" Bethany asked.

"Right," Jane said, "because an orphan means both parents are dead. If your mother or father is still alive, then you are not an orphan. Not yet."

Well, we had more serious things to talk about. All three of them had experienced some depression when a loved one died. It helped me to know I was not a total freak. Bethany had considered suicide. She teared up telling us about it. Jane's husband threatened divorce. He agreed to see a counselor with her but their marriage still needed help. We met another time or two in different restaurants. The conversations helped, I guess. On the other hand, I haven't seen Bethany or Jane since.

Weeks after Mom was gone, I began to regain some sensitivity to my home and family and realized that Annie had become my shadow. She had propped me up, and, also, collapsed into my breast after the funeral. We had a mother and daughter symbiosis.

Of course, the shop suffered. Oh - right, about my shop. How do I explain my shop? Artists, artisans of all kinds virtually infest the Hill Country. Therefore, it just seemed natural to me that there needed to be an art supply shop. There are Hobby Lobbies in New Braunfels and San Marcos and other places, as well as Michael's and Hancock's and stores like that. But I'm talking about a more specialized store for artists, not for hobbyists. I hire high school and college art students - they have to be art majors - and pretty much let them run the place. I have been doing this since Stephen started first grade. The store does well; people come from as far as San Angelo and Victoria. I spend as much time there as I choose and for a couple of months that was very little.

Now, with my son's life hanging by a thread I could sense the darkness returning that had captured me during mother's last weeks. I saw my depression as a deep, dark well, a prison to which I did not want to return. My son would need my strength to help him recover, not my weakness and dependency.

Well, actually, I had not been dependent on my boys after Mom's death. Stephen seemed pretty resilient and busy with his own life. We did not grieve together. George, on the other hand, disappeared for a brief time in a moody funk. I'm not sure what was going on but I know we, also, didn't grieve together.

## Chapter 14: Let's Go Home

Marie announced it was time for something to eat. "If we have a couple of hours with nothing else to do, let's go find some hamburgers."

"Or those tacos we never got to," offered Sylvester.

"Hey Mom," said Annie, "could we go home and change clothes? I'll bet we're going to be here all night."

### Annie

Standing in the hall, crying with Mom. It's like, here we are again. Sometimes with Marie or just the two of us. We can laugh or cry at the drop of a hat. We cried a lot when Mama Teresa was dying but we laughed too. Mom played "Piano Roll Blues" and Mama Teresa told her not to play songs like that because the men downstairs would be coming up to complain. Obviously, she was in one of her "alternate universe" phases. She did that occasionally toward the last. I said I thought the men downstairs liked that kind of music but she ignored me. Then she said for me to bring her the broom.

"Why do you want a broom?" I asked her.

"Bring it to me. I'll take care of you girls. Bring me the broom, Connie," she said. Sometimes she thought I was Mom. Then she goes, "And then you hide in the closet. When they get up here, I'll chase them off."

I looked at Mom like, what now? Mom goes, "Do you want me to crank the head of the bed up so you can get a good look at them?"

Mama Teresa looked around the bed and then at us. She put a hand to her head and laughed. "A lot of protection I'd be," she said and laughed some more. That time we laughed about her alternate universe experience.

## Chapter 15: Pastoral Visit

The phone was ringing the moment the Thompsons got home. Of course, Penny was all in a dither because the party had broken up and she had been left alone in the house. Ordinarily she is such a laid-back dog, but she could sense things were not right. She ran back and forth between the people she felt charged to protect like she was asking, "What's wrong? Where's George?"

Sylvester and Marie had driven one of the Thompsons' cars to the hospital and Dan had driven his parent's car, so everyone had transportation to go home. Connie had agreed they needed to change clothes and she wanted to bring some personal things back for an overnight stay. Arthur went along since there was no chance anyone could get in to see George for a while. Word had swept through town like a tornado. Apparently, each guest left the party and went home to call someone else.

The food had been put away but the house still smelled like a Mexican restaurant. Friends had pulled down party decorations and stacked them in a corner of the great room. The house had the feel of an abandoned party. Family members frowned from the bad taste it left.

Pastor Lance showed up while Arthur was talking to someone on the phone. He had driven into the parking lot at the hospital in time to watch the family drive out. He ran in, found Willow and asked about George and then he followed the Thompsons home.

Lance grabbed Arthur just as he hung up the phone.

## Annie

Stephen and I went to our rooms and changed clothes. Out of my party clothes and into jean shorts and a pink tee with a huge crimson carnation on it. Then I called Gwennie Tucker.

Gwennie is one of my very best friends in the entire world. She didn't come to the party because, well she and George don't hit it off that well. As soon as she heard my voice she said, "Oh my God, oh my God, Annie, what happened to George?

Everybody, just everybody is just crying and everything."

I told her we just did not know for sure, that he had been attacked and wasn't awake yet so we couldn't ask him. Then she goes, "This is just awful, it's the worst awful thing I've ever heard of."

"Yeah," I said. "The nurse told us he looks terrible."

"Was it, I mean did they do it because he's, you know, a gay person?"

"He's not gay!" I said. "Some people just have the wrong impression."

And she goes, "Really, Annie? Because, I dunno, lots of people say that - that George is gay."

"Like who? I've never heard anyone say that."

Now why did I say that? Because I hear it all the time from different girls at school. It just makes me so furious.

Sylvia and Sonita, the siss-sisters we called them, were walking home from school with me. I remember it was one of those early spring days when you wear a jacket to school in the cool morning but wish you didn't have to wag it home on a warm afternoon. I was telling them about going to a movie with Jasper Gumpfert and they kinda stopped and go like "Huh?" For a minute, I didn't know what that was about and then Sonita goes, "So you're not one of them?"

"One of what?"

"You know," goes Sylvia. "Like your brother, a homo."

Man, I went ballistic on them. "No, I'm not and neither is he!" I yelled.

"We didn't mean anything," they said. The siss-sisters were known for sticking their feet in their mouths and then having to apologize all day long.

"Don't say things like that," I told them.

"HELLO!" says Sonita. "Everybody knows that. We aren't making something up here."

"Everybody is totally wrong! Nobody knows George is gay. They just say that."

"Why do they say it if it isn't true?"

"Well, because they're stupid. I dunno. It's just wrong."

"Maybe you should talk to your brother about his image." Sylvia sometimes wants to give me advice. Anyway, that sort of thing happened every once in a while. So, I really had no business telling Gwennie that I had never heard anyone call George gay. She goes, "Whatever," and then asked if I wanted her to come over and we could, like talk. But I go, "Thanks, but no, because we're going back to the hospital pretty soon. But let's find some time to hang out tomorrow." She said we could do that.

## Chapter 16: Back to the Clinic

The two-fold purpose of coming home for the Thompsons was first to change out of party clothes and second to take time for a meal. This promised to be a long evening. Sustenance, nutrition, a protein-laced shot of fortitude would serve them well in the hours ahead. However, no one could conjure up an appetite, nor did anyone feel either interest or energy for fixing anything. Lance might have served them. Marie and Sylvester certainly would have. But the pastor left after a few minutes because of another obligation. He promised to drop by the clinic as soon as possible. Sylvester, Marie and Dan shot home with the same purpose as the Thompsons - change, eat, return - however with slightly more success. Marie forced sandwiches and chips on her men. Connie had only foraged in the pantry producing a box of energy bars, which she distributed with the explanation, "George won't mind sharing these." Before anyone could unwrap one she was pushing them toward the door and back to Caliche Hills' version of a hospital.

## Arthur

I hope when we get back to the clinic Syl
will still speak to me. I do not believe Syl or
I have ever hesitated to say to one another
exactly what was on our minds. We are that
kind of friends. I know him to the core and
he knows the color of my blood and bones.
There has never been any reason to hold
back anything. That is exactly why he said
what he said and that is exactly why I yelled
and swore at him. I guess it could not have
been otherwise nor should it be.

"ARE YOU OUT OF YOUR MIND? ARE
YOU OUT OF YOUR BLEEPING MIND?"

I was yelling. Yelling and cursing. I do not
do that. Fortunately, he and I had been the
only ones in the lounge. Yelling and cursing
at Sylvester of all people. Syl is my best
friend, just as our sons, Dan and George, are
best friends. Syl was only the messenger, but
I yelled at him. I hear myself yelling almost
anytime I have a minute to think. I probably
will dream of myself yelling.

"I think they were gay-bashing," Syl said. "I
think these creeps have figured George for a

homosexual and decided to beat him straight."

I kicked over my chair, bounced the table, and spilled several half empty Styrofoam cups.

Syl did not even stand up. He calmly motioned to me to sit down and grabbed a napkin to clean the table. I kicked my chair away and stomped over to a window to look outside. Not that I actually saw anything.

A nineteen-year-old boy cannot be a homosexual and his dad does not know anything about it! How could someone come up with this kind of garbage? He has a girlfriend, for crying out loud!

I tromped back to the table and dropped onto the chair. "Who ... where did you ... what in the world?"

Sylvester looked away. "What's the expression?" Then he looked at me, "Chill out, dude." I was not amused. "This is a theory, OK? And it really is a sound theory. I'm not saying that George is gay." I made a noise. "I'm saying someone could get that impression. It's an emotional issue. Some people go ballistic over it. You are going ballistic over it."

"I am not!"

"You are too, and you just proved the point. But, actually, that's not the point. This is an insane crime. In order for Smitty and his partner to work toward solving it they have to have some theories that explain what happened. Smitty knows George. Not real well, but he knows George."

"So, he ought to know better."

"Well, he knows enough to suspect."

"Suspect what? George is a man's man. He lettered in golf. He is a woodworker, for crying out loud, Syl. He just joined the Navy. And he's got a girlfriend. What do you say about that? Took her to the prom."

"Most of that proves nothing, Art. I'm sorry. Please hear what I am saying. I'm not saying anything against George."

"What are you saying, then?"

"I'm just presenting a picture that might explain - well, nothing can ever explain this senseless beating. But anyway. Homosexuals do all those things."

"Take girlfriends to the prom?"

Syl looked at me and then said, "I don't think George took her. I think she didn't go."

"Are you sure? George drove off headed for her house."

"Yes, I'm sure. She and I were in my garage creating large mounds of sawdust during the prom."

"Maybe so but still ..."

"Art," Sylvester laid a hand on my arm. "Art, George and Elspeth have been good friends for over a year. I have watched them in my shop. They talk about anything two people can find to cobble into a conversation. I guess I've never thought of them as boyfriend and girlfriend. Just friends."

"So you're saying ..."

"Nothing. I'm saying nothing. I'm just telling you what I know."

"So, my son got the life beat out of him because he's a wimp." I had to sit down.

"No," Syl said. "George is a strong young man. He is not a wimp and it probably took three or four guys to put him down."

## Chapter 17: A Two Car Trip

By the time Annie finished talking to Gwennie and got her clothes changed, Pastor Lance had left. She complained that she had wanted to say "hi" to him. In response, her father told her he had some place he had to be but he would see them later at the hospital. He then asked if she wanted to drive back to the hospital. Annie told him "No thanks." He said what he really meant was that they needed to take two cars so somebody in the family could return home earlier than the others. Annie guessed he meant that one parent or the other would spend the night. Annie drove Connie and Stephen rode with his dad.

On the way back to the hospital, Connie stared out the windshield. At one point she said, "I'll bet they didn't tell him how dangerous it would be."

"Huh?" said Annie.

That startled her mother. Annie mumbled something about one of Mama Teresa's alternate universes. Connie didn't say anything else until they were inside the hospital.

## Annie

One evening we rehearsed a play in our great room. George, Stephen, and I volunteered to do a play for our church. Once a quarter, the youth of all the churches in town meet for fellowship and we take turns providing a program or entertainment. We three had written and tested a play at our church and then took it to the community youth meeting. George played the father and I the mother of a typical Caliche Hills family. Stephen was the rebellious teen-age son. The gist of the play had Stephen wanting to try out new experiences like skateboarding and snorkeling but his "up-tight" parents imagined far worse activities. Stephen would come on stage and ask permission to go out; then George and I would confer, wringing our hands and moaning. After the test-run at our church we came home with a boatload of fresh ideas. At home, that evening during yet another rehearsal Stephen had made one of his innocent requests. I stood as tall as I could, arms crossed, eyebrows raised and said, "Steeeephen!" George stood for a moment (as the script directed him to do) and then, right as Stephen had a line, Mom goes, "Honey, don't you think that's a bit over the top?"

"What?" George and Stephen exclaimed together. I fell down laughing. When Dad laughed, Mom lightened up a bit and said, "Well, I guess you did sound like Mama Teresa, now that I think about it."

During the real performance, I got into an exaggerated "what have I done wrong" rhythm while George enjoyed pounding the kitchen table. The laughter goosed us into primordial ham acting. I know I enjoyed the whole experience, the planning, writing, rehearsing, and especially the acting. We grossly caricatured the teen/parent relationship. We knew it. We did it on purpose. It was so much fun because George played Dad and I played Mom with a lot of love. Stephen was just Stephen. And, that was just as much fun. We razzed Stephen as much as we did our parents. The thing is, it was very family. We all liked it. George played an "over the top" father of a teenage boy. He wasn't being hateful. We didn't ridicule our parents. He was good in that role. He will make a wonderful husband and father. Someday.

## Chapter 18: What Do You Do?

Walking back into the clinic Annie wrinkled her nose and muttered, "What do they clean hospitals with, formaldehyde?"

Past the reception area, they finally came to an apparent florist's shop. Potted plants, mostly ivy and carnations, filled several carts along the wall. The scent of blossoming life relieved Annie.

Elspeth was in the waiting room, still. She had not gone anywhere. According to her, no one had reported anything new about George. She looked slammed so Annie suggested they go get a soda. Sitting in the lounge, Annie turned to Elspeth. "Can I ask you something?"

"Sure, I guess," she smiled but it didn't last.

"What do you and George do?" That was not really what Annie wanted to ask but it was a start.

She leaned back and looked away. Then she smiled down at the table as if she was remembering something.

"Don't laugh," she says.

"Why would I laugh?"

"You would, I just know, anyone would."

Annie leaned toward her, eyebrows raised. "So what is it Elspeth? What do you guys do?"

"We dance."

"George doesn't dance." Then Annie did laugh.

"I told you." And she laughed, too.

Annie thought about it but could not believe it.

## Annie

Bushes outside the stadium flamed crimson as we walked through the gates. The oppressive humidity of summer released its grip on us and we could trot up the incline past the bleachers without breaking a sweat. Stephen ran ahead to find his compadres, Mom and Dad sauntered sedately and George pulled me along. Starting high school the next year gave him a fever of anticipation. I liked the grade I currently occupied but he hungered for the year to pass. At the game, I knew he was gonna twist his head off so as not to miss anything a high-schooler might do. We clomped up the concrete steps to the top row for the perspective. Here, we could see the goal posts and chalk stripes, the bright colors of the bands and the teams, the acrobatics of the cheerleaders and the antics of children playing their own brand of ball along the sidelines. I liked it because you couldn't smell the players in the second half. Here, you could hear the men in the press box asking each other who made that block or where did you move the ashtray, the band director yelling at the drum section to watch him during the playing of the next march, the jokers just below us making up their own words while the cheerleaders hollered, "Hit 'em again, harder, harder."

Of course, we didn't spend the whole game up there. We ran down the steps to catch up with some friends headed for the refreshment stand. Guys pushed at other guys and rattled on about who knows what. Gals caught up on their special secrets. And sometimes, like in this particular memory, George and I ended up back on the top row trying to figure out whether we were winning. We were more into the half time than the game. The Caliche Hills marching band rocks. They are so awesome. I said that to George. Then I asked if he was considering playing the trumpet.

"Why would I do that?" he frowned.

"So you can march in the band. That would be so totally awesome!"

He turned and just stared at me. "Are you out of your ever-lovin' mind? Why would I want to march in the band?"

I go, "Why wouldn't you? That has to be the coolest ..."

He just laughed.

I pushed his shoulder. "Come on. You would like to march in the band. I know you would."

He moved toward me and kinda squinched up his shoulders. "No I would not," he goes. "I don't have rhythm."

"Whadda ya mean?"

"I can't march. I don't want to march in the first place and anyway I don't care anything about keeping time with music."

Anyway, that's what he told me then.

More recently, he told me he joined the Navy instead of going to college because he wasn't ready for college.

"Not ready for college!" I didn't believe it. "You're more ready for college than anyone in your graduating class."

"No. I am not, Annie. I'm not sure who I am. I need to find that out. I want the kind of disciplined regimen that makes a kid into a man."

"Why not the Marines?"

"I get to choose the discipline."

I pouted. My immaturity never won me anything but it felt good anyway.

## Chapter 19: Dancing

"Where do you go?" Annie asked. "There's no place around here to dance. Austin?"

"We go to Mrs. Bailey's garage. Last summer we cleaned it out as a high school good neighbor project and she said we could use it anytime. So we brought in a CD player and, well, we dance."

"But George can't dance." She absolutely knew this for a fact.

"Yeah, he can. Not much at first. He knew how to move to a beat. He knew a box step and some waltz steps. Learned those in maybe fifth or sixth grade."

"Oh yeah. But he didn't like it."

"No, he didn't. He told me that. I had earphones on and was doing some Salsa moves while we were cleaning the garage. I tried to coax George into some of that but he blew me off. Said he had no interest. Dan and a couple of girls were there and somebody had a radio. We started doing the Electric Glide - a line dance. George went along and, I dunno, I guess he decided it wasn't so bad."

"So you guys and Dan and some others go over to Mrs. Bailey's and dance. Why don't I know about this?"

"No. No, no, no. Just George and me. Several people were dancing during the cleanup. But - you see, only the two of us were talking to Mrs. Bailey later and - well, I dunno, maybe Dan was with us. But only me and George followed up."

"Do you do this a lot? I mean, I don't get how come nobody knows about this. And I know that nobody knows about it because I don't know about it and if I don't know about it, nobody does."

She leaned back and sighed. "No. Not a lot. But every couple of weeks we find time to go over there. We don't play anything loud and there are not a whole lot of lights on. It doesn't draw attention."

"So, what? You fox trot and waltz?"

She laughed. "Sometimes. We mostly swing and salsa."

"George can do that?"

"I had to teach him."

"Wow." She still could not believe her brother George dancing.

Then Annie said, "Wait a minute! Wait just a big honking minute."

"What?"

"The two of you don't date? These are not dates? Who do you think you're fooling here?"

A look of fear crossed her face. She sat up straight. "Listen, Annie. Do not tell anyone about this? Please! Don't!"

"But Elspeth. Don't you know what people are saying about George? And maybe about you too, I dunno. I mean, gays don't dance with girls. This proves something."

"Please, Annie." Tears came to her eyes. This was off the charts. It made no sense. "You don't understand. It's not a date. We don't dance as boyfriend and girlfriend or anything like that. In fact, that's why we can dance together. We love the music and the movement and we can enjoy dancing without all that stuff that goes on with a couple. We aren't two people looking to make out. We enjoy the dance. And nobody can know about this because - they just can't!"

"Okay," I said. "Okay, I sure won't tell anyone because I don't understand. How can I explain something I don't understand?"

"Please, Annie." She grabbed my arm. "George would kill me if he knew I told you. He doesn't - neither one of us want people to know about this."

"Why the big secret? Okay, if George doesn't want you to tell, then - I can appreciate this - you told me just between the two of us. But why?"

"Because, just because." She was crying now. We sat.

"We're a whole lot confused. I'm confused, anyway. I'm not interested in boys. George and Dan . . . I don't know how to say this." She bit her lip. "They aren't boy boys."

"Huh?"

"They're woodworking buddies. And that's as far as it goes with Dan. George is also my dance partner and *confidente*."

"*Confidente*?"

"*Si*, we confide in each other."

After a moment, Annie's tongue got dry. She realized she had been sitting there with her mouth open.

"Elspeth," she said. "My head is swimming. If it's all right with you, let's talk about this some other time. And I do want to talk about it some more - just the two of us. Maybe I can also be your *confidente*."

Again she smiled. "You would be my *guia*."

"Oh, yeah, I know that one. Your guide? I don't think so."

Elspeth looked toward the hall and said, "Kinda empty, isn't it?"

Annie nodded. The people of the village talked about their "Big Clinic," meaning CHH. The Caliche Hills Hospital, however, was not really even a small hospital. Annie remembered seeing one other cubicle in the intensive care ward where George lay. There might be twenty rooms in all.

"Yeah, empty," Annie said.


## Elspeth

George would stand right foot behind the left with his left hand extended and a slight bow of his head - an invitation to dance. I would lean my head back slightly, and arch my back, reaching out my right hand to accept his invitation. He would lead me forward into a twirl and then pull me to him and we would dance. The first dance would be a rhumba. A sensual, physical, moving and gliding. I would twirl and float and glide. We loved swing steps but what I enjoyed most was teaching George to Salsa. He was so funny at first. Graceful and smooth, but at the same time displaying a fifth-grade stiffness and formality. He knew a basic box step and that was good. From there we moved to the rhumba. That required getting your hips into the action. No way. Not at first. But I convinced him. "There's no one but you and me," I told him. "Let's be movie stars. We're Jennifer Grey and Patrick Swayze in Dirty Dancing!" That sparked him but he really wanted to be Kevin Bacon from Footloose.

I complained one time that there were no other opportunities to dance. He knew what I meant. "Who would you dance with if not here with me?" he asked. Nobody. He knew that, but he asked me one time if there were some girls I could dance with. "Isn't that what happens at pajama parties?" How would I know? Most of the girls here will not have anything to do with me. I told him they must hate me, or something. Anyone else, even Dan, would have said, "Naw, they don't hate you." But George knew. George told me about a golf match where some students from the other school involved followed him through his round and jeered at him.

"Really?" I said.

"Yeah," he said. "It's like they hated me. I guess that's what hit me so hard. Their eyes. Their eyes hated me. They shot lightening at me. I was frightened. I could not play. I duffed more shots than ever. I've never seen such hatred. How could they hate me with such vehemence? I didn't even know them."

"That must have been awful."

"Yeah, I really felt queer."

I looked at him funny. "You felt like a queer."

He gave a startled laugh. "No, I didn't mean that. Not the way it sounded. But some of them did call me that."

"So, this was what? A Freudian slip?"

"No," he insisted. "I just meant I felt weird, unusual. I wasn't saying anything. I wouldn't use that word like that."

"It's all right," I said. "I know how you feel." And I did. I knew that he accepted my questions about my sexuality, because questions were all I had. I probably am lesbian but I am still not sure I want to say that. I've told George that and he's okay about it. I told Dan, too. He just said, "So? I wasn't going to ask you for a date anyway."

## Chapter 20: ICU

The room was cool and dimly lit. The patient provided the centerpiece for this ensemble but he was covered in white and surrounded by electrical devices. With his head shrouded in bandaging, an arm equally covered, one had little perception of the person lying here. The doctor reluctantly agreed with Nurse Carroll that the family could have brief access to their loved one. The emphasis clearly on brief. "And you stay in here with them," he warned. "One at a time. Two minutes each." She nodded and they both left the room.

### Arthur

Sometime later, I was not too conscious of the rate at which time passed. Time actually seems irrelevant. Anyway, the nurse, Willow Carroll, came in and said we could go see George briefly one at a time. Connie immediately said Annie and Stephen ought to go first. The kids just as quickly declined and said she should go first and before

anyone offered a different opinion, Connie
was out the door. She came back in about
two minutes and collapsed into my arms.
"He looks awful," she cried, "just awful." I
nodded at Stephen and Annie and they
moved off down the hall together. When
they came back, Stephen just nodded his
head and said, "Pretty bad." Connie and
Annie sat in a corner together.

### Annie

They told us we could go into the intensive
care room and spend two minutes with
George. Stephen gestured for me to go in
first and I rushed through the door, but just
as I entered the room, I stopped. I was afraid
of what I would find. An antiseptic smell
attempted to cover odors of blood and
ugliness. Gauze, sheets, and bandages
wrapped all around him. He looked like a
ghost already. I couldn't even tell if he was
breathing, a little plastic tubey thing was
strapped around his head under his nose. He
was wearing a helmet bandage and
something beeped the whole time I was in
there. I rubbed his arm and whispered to him
but he made no response. I didn't cry until I

116

got back to the waiting room. Then Mom and I couldn't help it. We just hugged and wept.

I wish he could have answered my question.

## Stephen

Dan's parents took us up to the waiting room. I'm not sure why. It's not that big of a room and looks like a dentist's office. Creepy. But Annie and my folks were there so it made sense to go up. Someone said we could go see George one at a time. Mom went first and then Annie and I walked down the hall together. At the door, I stepped aside so she could go in first. She looked like a ghost when she came out. I soon saw why. I wouldn't have recognized him if I had met him on the street. Sure, met him on the street, like who's that guy in the hospital bed with his head all wrapped? Man, he looked awful.

Willow told me to talk to him but I could not think - I mean, what do you say to your unconscious brother who never met a mess he couldn't clean up and now he's the mess. His face was all puffy and discolored. I just stood there and then I grabbed his hand. One hand had a needle in the back of it connected to some bottle but the hand closer to me was free. He didn't respond. I wanted him to squeeze back at me. I tried to will him to squeeze. An oxygen mask covered some of his face. It was bad, really bad. That's what I said when I went back into that cramped, over-heated waiting room. Maybe I should have tried to be more upbeat, I dunno. When I looked down at his hand, I noticed his knuckles were scraped. Both hands. I checked the other one, too. He must have fought back. That was when I finally found some words. "You're the man," I told him. "You're the man."

What if he wasn't going to get out of this? George had always found the way to get out, go forward, or rescue the situation. That's what I like about him so much. I was on the bag for him at a meet where his drive was almost lost behind a tree in thick grass and no shot to the green. I told him his only play was to pitch the ball backwards into the fairway. His only clear shot was backwards. Any attempt toward the green would just get him into more trouble. He was facing bogey no matter what, but a stupid heroic shot would cost more shots. He agreed with me - more or less. Instead of pitching backwards to the left into our fairway, he hit the ball forward to the right into the adjoining fairway, hit it close to the hole from there and actually salvaged par. That was an equally clear way to go. I just couldn't think broader than the fairway we were supposed to be playing. That was George, though. Calmly seeing the larger picture. No panic. Somebody beat George with a club. Did George panic then? Whoever it was at least had a bloody nose.

I realized the window I was staring through was now reflecting a picture of me. Darkness had settled outside as well as in the intensive care unit where my brother lay unconscious.

## Arthur

I almost ran down the hall but stopped abruptly at the door to ICU. I hardly recognized that our pastor's wife, Willow, was the nurse standing just inside the door. When she saw me, she opened the door and took my arm. "He isn't awake but you should talk to him, Art." She led me into a room, a cubicle, where George lay hooked to life support. A large bandage swathed his head. His face was swollen and almost completely black. His right hand looked like a huge avocado: green, black, and puffy. I put my hands on his left shoulder and arm. He felt cool. I wanted to yell, "Who did this to you? Who? And why?" Instead, I spoke quietly. "You're going to be just fine, son. The doctors and nurses will have you up and around in no time. We're all praying for you, son." I felt Willow's hand on my back. I could not see how to get out of there but she guided me through the door.

When I got back to the waiting room, I told Connie what I had said to George. "I know we need to be praying for him, but right now, what I want to do is yell," I told her.

"Yell at whom?"

"At God, I guess. At whoever did this. I do not know. Just yell."

Sylvester came over and put his arm around my shoulder. "Let's go out back and yell, then. You and me."

"No," I said. "I'm not really going to do that. Not right now anyway."

120

I am going to do that someday. I am going to find a fair sized hill and I'm going to scream at the top of my lungs so they'll hear me in Oklahoma, Louisiana, New Mexico and Mexico City. I'm not going to make a speech. I doubt if I will even say one intelligible word. I'm just going to yell.

## Chapter 21: Something Random

After each Thompson had gone in to see George, Dan asked if he could go in. Arthur cleared it with Nurse Carroll and Dan managed to spend a couple of minutes in there. Stephen could not tell where Dan's face left off and his white tee shirt began when he came back. Sylvester grabbed Stephen's arm, pushed Dan into the hall, and said, "Let's get something to drink." Stephen sighed; relieved to be heading back toward the snack bar. The three sat in a corner by a window where Sylvester asked what they thought. Stephen shrugged as if to indicate he did not want to say what he thought. He was trying to forget what he thought. Dan told his father it was brutal. They sat and looked out the window or at the floor.

Finally Dan asked his dad a question and Sylvester just looked at him.

"What was that?" Stephen asked.

Dan shifted toward him. "Were they from around here?"

"Who? The guys who did George?"

"Yeah, those guys. Do you think they were from around here?"

"No way, man. Nobody from the Hills would do something like that."

"I'd have to agree with Stephen," said Sylvester.

Dan nodded his head and turned back toward the table where he sat. "That's what I want to believe, but I dunno. It had to be someone who knew George well enough to have a bad opinion about him."

"That's kind of what the cops think," said Sylvester. "But it might just be something random."

"Ha!" Dan slapped the table. "Nothing random about it. Dad, I told Stephen this, I drove out by there on the way here. They spray painted the fence. They wrote 'Fag' over George's body. They knew him - or thought they did."

"Sounds like they were careless and stupid. They've probably left all sorts of clues. The police will find them."

"Probably," Stephen answered, "but how does that help George? You know what? I just don't think ..." He had to stop for a minute.

Sylvester asked, "What do you think, Stephen?"

"I don't really want to think any more."

Dan ducked his head. "He does look pretty bad."

## Annie

After I saw George in ICU, I just wanted to crawl in a dark corner somewhere. Back in the waiting room we cried and hugged and blubbered about how bad he looked. Then I did find a corner, hugged myself, and tried to figure how this day went downhill so fast.

I was not that excited about George going off to be a sailor. I was more help thinking about how to celebrate his senior year. I wish I could make grades like George. He always made honor society. He wasn't the valedictorian or anything but he pulled down a lot of A's. If he wasn't at home studying, he was playing golf or sawing and sanding boards. We have wooden vases and bookends all over the place. Mom and Dad have a small bookcase in the living room that George made for them. George made Stephen a wooden thing, I don't know what you call it, but it's a box with a bottom and four sides and a handle going from the front end to the back end. Stephen puts his smaller gardening tools in it. On the wall in my room, opposite the window there's a white shelf with scallopy edges carved by a router. It's sort of small and simple except when you look at it real close, you see it's really ornate or elaborate. That shelf is my favorite thing in the room.

The worlds of golf and woodworking revolve in different solar systems from where I live. So, I don't see George when he's in one of those galaxies. Studying sometimes brings us together. He likes to tutor me, not that I need the help. Honestly, I do all right. I make good grades on my own. Still, I enjoy picking his brain. I can get off on the way his mind works. So, sometimes I'll ask him what he thinks the teacher wants from me. That almost guarantees forty minutes of brotherly advice. Although he is sixteen months older, I finished my junior year as he closed out as a senior. Fourteen months separate Stephen and me. So we have stair stepped through school, one of us entering the grade another just vacated.

Gossip is the other thing that brings George into my world. Not that we gossip, no sir, not George. No, it's what I hear about George at school. This little sister has always had girls my age and older asking about my "hunky" brother. When they get cold-shouldered and see that no one else can attract his attention either, they say unflattering things.

The kindest thing anyone said was when Louisa Delgado asked me if my brother was studying for the priesthood. Next up on a scale of offensiveness are the girls who huff about how conceited George is. Full of himself, nose-in-the-air, too good for us mere mortals, are some of the nicer comments. Anyone could have already guessed the worst remarks. One girl I could gladly slap silly asked me who George's boyfriend was. Sometimes girls say things directly to me. There are girls who complain to each other intending for me to overhear. A few times I have caught snatches of whispering I'm pretty sure aren't intended for anyone to hear.

I never said anything to George about the rumors and stuff. I mean, how do you ask your brother if he knows people think he is homosexual? I guess someone could say that if you and your brother are tight, you can say anything.

George does stuff with Elspeth but nobody much knows about that. And, really, most of the time it's George, Dan, and Elspeth. None of that amounts to what you would call a date. A date, pffft, yeah, right. George just never uses the word and Elspeth can go ballistic about it. I really rarely see that much of her but we have had some good talks about, oh, I dunno, why people get so jacked up about a girl trying to make something of herself. You know, like once I wanted to be a rock star; no, seriously, I did. Not for long but anyway it's not such a crazy idea. I play the piano pretty well and I can carry a tune. Rock stars don't have to have great voices. I know it's a bogus idea and I got off it pretty quick but what flips me is the people who took off on me because I was a girl wanting to be a rock star. So anyway, Elspeth was asking what's up with my music, we got to talking, and she got all melty over Selena. Her favorite Selena song was *Como La Flor*. She told me she played Selena's CDs at night and fantasized she was still alive and doing concerts in Caliche

Hills with Elspeth in the front row. Well, what got her started on Selena was this whole thing about a woman in business and being a successful popular music star. But don't think that we spend a lot of time together. I mean, if she's here, she's with George and they are going, "Who says?" or "Who knows?" They just have issues about know-it-alls I guess.

Don't get the wrong idea. George is not against dating. He's just not interested himself. So does that mean he is gay? I don't think so. No, he's for dating if you're into that kind of thing. Not that he and I talked about it much. I sort of felt that my boyfriends were none of his business. But when Jimmy Leicester asked me to go to a dance and I told everybody about it at dinner that evening, George was the first to say, "You go, girl!"

I want to tell him thanks for that. I mean he has been hard on me but never mean and sometimes he just knows what I'm thinking or feeling. At the time, I don't want him inside my brain. But, what if that's never going to happen again? Get out of that bed and walk, George. Where is Jesus when you need him?

If he pulls out of this, I would be glad to listen to any kind of trash that girls want to dish in the locker room. I mean, that is no big deal. But, how could someone just bash in your head because you look or act different. Mom has never known what George put up with. Well, maybe, a little. Elspeth came over one day and George wasn't there and we hung out a while and Mom saw us and she goes, "Elspeth, George says you don't date. What does he mean by that? You two have gone out together." And Elspeth goes, "Yeah, Miz T. We hang together a lot but I'm not his girlfriend." Elspeth told me she talked to Mom about that later and tried to explain to her that "friend" did not have to mean romance or whatever. She said it almost made her sick to her stomach for a boy to run his hand across her shoulder or brush her hand in a suggestive way. George and Dan, they never touched her like that. George seemed to understand that better than Dan. Dan just does not pay attention. He misses a lot.

This was out back of the house. We had crashed in our lawn chairs and were watching the light fade, and I was humming *Moonlight Serenade*, which is a cool piano piece and Elspeth asked me about the song. I told her the chord progression, how smooth I thought it was, and then told her the words - the ones I could remember. She goes, "That's kind of a love song, isn't it?" "Yeah," I said. "But what good is a love song if you hate men?" That got her going. She said she doesn't hate anyone. She just is not interested in a boyfriend.

It had gotten seriously dark by then. I couldn't see her face so I suppose she couldn't see mine. That may have helped her talk to me. Well, actually, not talk to me for a while. Then she said, "George and I have gotten into this several times and he asked me if I thought I was maybe a lesbian."

"Are you?" I asked. I don't always think too much before I say things. But, I wasn't all screaming or "No you can't be!"

"I dunno," she said. "How do you know something like that? I don't have a barcode anywhere on my body that you can scan and it comes out: Female homosexual." She told me she didn't think she wanted to be a lesbian but she had a bad history with men. She would not expand on that and I didn't push. I wish now I had asked what George said about his sexuality. I still can, I suppose. Would that be insensitive right now? Maybe not.

## Chapter 22: Confined

In the ebb and flow of torturous waiting, family and friends can be spread all over the place one minute and crammed together in a small cubicle the next. By twos or threes, all of George's family and friends filtered back into the surgical waiting room. The air conditioning system barely kept the room below stifling. Stephen leaned toward the door as if he would leave and was about to wave at Dan and Elspeth when he thought he saw someone in the hall. Maybe they were about to learn something. He and Dan exchanged looks that suggested a "wait-and-see and then we'll bolt", agreement.

## Connie

I saw Dr. Sauerwein coming toward the waiting room. He certainly had been a lifesaver many times over. Now there's a family doctor! I remember he had once practiced in a small little office off the square. His wife was the nurse and her sister helped them out as receptionist/bookkeeper.

Later he found the financial backing to build this small clinic/hospital on the edge of town. He succeeded in keeping the atmosphere of a close, caring practice in the new building. It was Dr. Sauerwein, after all, who diagnosed my first "illness."

That was daybreak for my dreams. "It must be a stomach virus," I had told him, quite sure that it was my job to give the doctor the diagnosis.

"Do you really think so?" he smiled.

"What else do you suppose it could be?" I innocently asked.

"Well, Connie, either you have the Mongolian heebie-jeebies, or crankitis sour stomachus, or just possibly you might actually be pregnant."

What a joyous surprise! I had no idea. A listing of all the things we didn't know then would fill a metropolitan library. Later, with Annie and Stephen, I knew immediately that we had another little one on the way.

"If it's a girl," I told Art, "I want to name her Charlotte Ann for mother's sisters."

"What if we have a boy?" he asked.

"Arthur Regis, Jr."

"No way," he laughed. "No way am I going to tag a son of mine with the junior label. We then would end up with grandson Trip or Trey, followed by Quad and Quint, and who knows. I just don't want that."

"Okay, what then?"

"How about Theodore Geisel Thompson?"

"Huh? Where'd you get that?"

"We could call him Dr. Seuss."

"Oh, Art! Don't be silly."

"C'mon Connie. You know you love Dr. Seuss and you've always said that we would read *The Cat in the Hat* and *Green Eggs and Ham* ..."

"But," I interrupted, "I never said we'd name our children after him. Next you would want to name a child Horton the Who Thompson."

"Horton heard a Who. He wasn't the Who."

"Who cares?" I answered.

Finally, Art got serious enough to share a memory. As a teenager, he had read a biography of the Methodist evangelist George Whitefield. Whitefield greatly influenced American history with his participation in a great awakening or some sort of revival movement. I'm not that familiar with the story myself but I saw that the mere mention of Whitefield's name stirred profound memories for Art. That settled it. We had a name for our boy.

George, the eldest, is the pacesetter, just as his mother's dream framed him to be. Charlotte Ann - Annie to the rest of the world - still purses her lips and determines not to be like him, and succeeds remarkably at rowing her own canoe, but she excels at whatever piques her interest. Don't tell her how much her achievements remind you of George. She will not hear it.

George was at his most headstrong telling me he was not ready for college. Not mature enough! Can you believe that? He needed experience to shape him and point him before he settled on a major or a career. I guess he was already thinking military last winter.

Now Stephen - Arthur tagged him Stephen Andrew – Stephen for the first Christian martyr in the book of Acts and Andrew, the first apostle and the patron saint of Scotland. Stephen always wanted to be just like George, but he is not. He follows George around, or he did when they were younger.

He really takes a different route now, although sometimes in George's footsteps. To the best of my memory, golf is the only thing they have in common. For instance, Stephen has no interest in woodworking. His brother spends hours at Sylvester's garage carving, sanding, and shellacking or whatever it takes to bring home beautiful knick-knacks and furniture to his mother. Stephen would rather dig up a tree in the back yard and plant it in front of the house.

# Chapter 23: The Doctor Walks

Dr. Sauerwein bore his responsibilities gravely. He would trade telling a husband and grandparents, "It's a boy!" or "She's a beautiful girl!" every single time over making this announcement. Nevertheless, he had chosen the job, warts and all. Two steps out the door, left fifteen feet down the hall, then right. There was time to pull the stethoscope off his neck and shove it into a pocket. He adjusted the knot on his tie. Younger doctors never wore ties. He believed the dignity of the profession called for it. If ever an occasion called for a dignified carriage, this one did. How could it happen? We were so meticulous! And now Winchell was seeing to another emergency. Hands on, Winchell was good. Face to face, like right now, he was no help. The weight in Sauerwein's heart fought against this march but muscle memory charged his legs forward. Quickly through the pain, he had always believed, was the best way.

# Arthur

We had been back in the family lounge - that is what the clinic called it - for about a half an hour when I picked out Dr. Sauerwein coming toward the lounge. Dr. Sauerwein has been our family's physician since before Connie was pregnant with George. A thin, tall, white-haired man, now late-fifties, he was extended family to us. We had seen him briefly earlier when he came by to tell us that Dr. Winchell was an excellent surgeon and would take good care of George and again to report with Winchell on George's condition. Although he was not the emergency room doctor, I think he was involved in whatever they were doing for our son. I know he had looked in on George several times.

My first instinct was that Doc was coming to give us a progress report. Maybe he was going to tell us that George was awake and we could go see him. However, the stern expression on his face told me otherwise. Just as he got to the door I took a step backward and muttered, "Oh, no."

When the door opened, every head turned toward him. There was a long deep silence.

"I'm sorry," he said.

There is something wrong and unnatural about outliving your child. Oh, do not give me that stuff about all through history parents had dozens of kids because of high infant mortality rates and the odds that less than half of the world's children survive to maturity. It is wrong and unnatural when your son dies when you are still a young or middle-aged adult. It is wrong!

George will distinguish himself in military service to his country. Returning from duty, he will go to college financed by a golf scholarship and the government. After graduation and fueled by my encouragement a short internship in a computer store sets up an entrepreneurial jump into his business. He has a future! Marriage and grandchildren for Connie and me. Family reunions! It is all out there. It just is not right to cut down a young man with such promise. It is wrong!

All right! So other parents lose children. There is a park in town with a brick sidewalk bearing the names of young people who died during their high school years. So what! Those deaths were wrong, too, and that does not make it any less painful or less wrong for George to die.

"No," I told doc. "No." I muttered it several times. He needed to go back and check George's pulse. This time I did not yell. Part of me stood somewhere in outer space staring at a void as another piece of my mind repeated it is really true, he really died. I am a soulless, empty cardboard refrigerator box.

I pulled Connie to me and felt her sobs rock me and echo throughout my emptiness. It is wrong!

I hugged Annie holding her up. She felt so limp as if all of her life had been sucked out of her. Marie helped me fold Connie and Annie into one another. Stephen held this blank stare, an uncomprehending vacancy. I wrapped an arm around his head. "We have to help each other through this, guy," I whispered into the top of his head. He did not speak or cry. Minutes later, he sat with his head in his hands.

What happened? How could this be! Doc just frowned and shook his head. Maybe he tried to explain. I could not hear it.

Willow must have called her husband. Lance burst into the room, his eyes wide. "It is just wrong!" I told him. He did not correct me. He just said he was so sorry about George. He was sorry that he had left because of an appointment. He wished he had been here with us when we got word of George's death. Actually, he did not say very much. He listened to me blow off steam. Afterward I worried that he might have felt I was blaming him for my son's death. Well, it is wrong. Someone should hear me say this. It is just wrong.

Maybe deep in the heart of a tragedy is the time to talk about important ideas. Maybe, when your heart beats so violently you know it will tear its way out of your chest, maybe that is the time to question everything. I just want someone to agree with me. When your son dies, it is wrong!

## Chapter 24: The Mortician

There had been explanations. Something about a missed leak, a torn something. Just words, confusing, contradictory, forgotten words.

The mortician came. The man everyone sees at different funerals. Arthur thought they might have met although he could not remember that. The mortician's face was waxy fat. His words fell out of his mouth and soaked into the carpet. "Now what?" Arthur asked. He later commented that he had made more sense out of asking old ladies to describe their computer problems. Somehow, the two made an appointment to meet the next day to work out funeral arrangements. He, the mortician, was part of a muddle of people who apologized for George having died, and offered condolences and expressed a willingness to help. The family must have felt like everyone in the hospital shook a hand or one-arm hugged them and made the same speech three times. Stephen looked like a large pump had drained all his blood from his face. Annie's face shone of tears. Dan walked around with a tight grip on himself, squeezing himself in a perpetual hug. Marie positioned herself between Connie and Annie and kept both hands and frequently both arms on them. Arthur knew that Sylvester was close, not always next to him, but close. Connie remembered focusing on Elspeth's back moving quickly through the door, running away from the pain.

## Stephen

My stomach hurts. How does that happen?

At some point Dan asked me, "Do you know about the time he got beat up at a golf tournament?"

Maybe we were outside when he said that.

I said, "No way!"

"Yeah he did. He was playing in a tournament just outside San Antonio and doing rather well. He said there were five guys from that high school our football team creamed in last year's state semi-finals. The coach told them to take advantage of the driving range before they went home. Lots of new Titlist balls. The locker room was like a maze of, well, lockers. George got confused and turned the wrong direction, away from the door, it seems."

"Did you play that tournament?"

"Nah, don't you remember? Coach only took three guys. You and me, we didn't make it."

"Oh, right. So, how do you know about this?"

"He told me in our garage. Just him and me. Elspeth wasn't there and Dad was off buying saw blades or something. George's eyes were focused on something I couldn't see. He began to sweat as he told me his story. He said five of them came from nowhere. Names. They called him names. He said they hurt him. 'Don't hit his face!' someone shouted. Tall, ugly kid. George said he couldn't putt. 'Don't hit his face! No obvious bruises on this fag,' he said."

"That's just criminal! How come I didn't know this?"

"He avoided you and Annie and tried to avoid your mom when he got home. When she asked about the tournament, he lied. 'Fine,' he said. 'Just a little tired. We won second,' he said. 'Just tired,' he lied."

## Chapter 25: Funeral Day

Pastor Lance insisted the Thompsons come to the funeral early so Connie pushed until they got there earlier than early. Annie complained that it was a total bummer because what are you going to do at church all dressed up and nobody is there? Elspeth popped her head into the Sunday school room where Stephen and Annie were kicking around and joined them. The two girls traipsed outside but didn't stay because, as Annie put it, "It is getting like hotter than The Place You Don't Want to Go There." The sanctuary sat empty. The family was avoiding the sanctuary as if it was off limits before the service. So obviously, Elspeth tugged Annie in and led her to a back row. They sat where Annie and Stephen always sat so Annie immediately called it, "home base." Elspeth wanted to know how Annie was doing and how her Mom and Dad were holding up and Annie asked the same thing about her. The scent of flowers all across the front of the room overpowered them. A man in a jumpsuit came in with more flowers. He fussed a little with a couple of sprays and then left.

## Elspeth

Annie sneezed as the florist walked by us with an elaborate - well, gaudy - spray. I laughed and said something about giving her flowers might not be the most romantic thing to do. We just stared at the front of the sanctuary. For no reason, I started talking about George and Dan.

"George loved to give Dan a hard time about asking girls for a date," I said. "Actually there was only one girl Dan ever considered asking. Sometimes they would get into hassling each other and they would forget I was there sanding wood with them. Maybe that was it. Maybe they just were comfortable with me being there."

"Makes sense," Annie said.

"Dan wore a plaid flannel lumberjack shirt all winter long. Actually, I think he owned two or three that looked about the same. They were awful. I would tell him Paul Bunyan wouldn't be caught dead in one of those. George preferred V-neck sweaters worn over cotton shirts. Dan never wore sweaters. Well, that is, except for his golf letter-sweater, the one clothing item both guys agreed on. Dan was complaining because his creative writing teacher made him tuck in his shirttail. 'She's gonna die she's losing so much blood!' he said. I had no idea what he thought he meant."

Annie grunted.

I nodded. "George took him on. 'Whatta you know about periods?'

" ' 'Bout as much as you do.' said Dan."

I raised my shoulders and deepened my voice.

" 'Yeah, right. You don't have a sister and your mother never tells you anything."

"George said that to Dan?"

"Yeah. They were going after each other. 'Who wants to get their sex education from their mother?' Dan said. And then he goes, 'Besides, what I don't know I can learn from Tracye.'

" 'Thanks a lot,' I interrupted. You'd think they didn't even know I existed.

" 'Yeah,' said Dan, 'I guess there are some parts of being female you can't avoid.' "

"I threw a block of wood at him."

"I hope you hit him someplace vital." Annie sat up. "Tracye? Did Dan ever date her?"

"Right. That's what George wanted to know. Dan said he hadn't paid her way to a movie or something. But they had 'gone places, done things together.' I looked him up and down. 'Gone places, done things - what does that mean?' I asked him.

"He stomped over and glared at me nose to nose.

" 'Well, it means I asked her to go to the senior prom with me and she said yes.'

"George asked him when that had happened. Then Dan turned it back on George and asked who he intended to take to the prom."

Annie turned toward me. "George didn't take anyone to the prom."

"I know. Dan made a noise and started a little chicken dance. I whacked his arm. 'Cut it out,' I said. He ducked away from me and wagged his finger under George's nose. 'Sooner or later, good bud, you're gonna have to ask somebody for a date.'

"Later, I got George aside and told him, 'Don't even think about it. I am not going to that prom. 'I know,' he grinned. 'I wouldn't want you to have to buy a dress.' "

"The two of you were pretty easy together," Annie said. "You had a comfortable relationship."

"I guess we did. The difference between George and me is that I'm more vocal about my sexuality. I've told both guys that I have some questions and maybe I just am a lesbian. George was willing to admit to me one time that he understood about having questions but he never said anything more specific.

"He told me about being in Sunday school just before I moved to town when the teacher got a little off on an X-rated lesson. 'David was a great man and a great king but he had his weaknesses.' That was the build-up from Mr. Righteous - I don't know his name, just what George called him."

"I know who you're talking about. He left and went to some other church. I never had him as a teacher."

"You should have heard George mimic him. Maybe you did?"

I raised my eyebrows but Annie shook her head.

I sat up and waved my arms. "David had his weaknesses and Mr. Righteous told the class exactly what they were. David lusted after Bathsheba, stole another man's wife and then had the man killed. He explained that it just isn't right to kill another man to get his wife. One of the Grainger brothers asked Mr. Righteous ..."

"When is it right to kill another man?" Annie interrupted me with the punch line.

I laughed and pointed at her.

"Somebody quipped, 'You can trade your pick-up for his wife; you just don't kill him.' Everybody laughed at that. Then George imitated Mr. Righteous as he put his elbows on his knees and leaned toward the boys and began to talk in his shut-up-I'm-dead-serious voice. 'Boys,' George rumbled in mock seriousness, 'You young men are old enough to learn some deep fundamental truths about sex. God has one special girl for each one of you.' George told me, 'The teacher looked hard at every one of us, leaving me to last and, I swear, he looked at me twice as long as any other boy in the room.' "

I could see the look in George's eyes at that moment. Annie took my hand.

I squeezed her hand and leaned back against the pew.

"Thanks for the story, Elspeth. Each of us has a piece of George. It's good to share."

## Chapter 26: Girl Talk

"Teach me to salsa," Annie said. She hadn't thought about it. It simply popped out of her mouth. Elspeth laughed. "No. Really. I want to learn. And it would be, you know, neat to carry on something you shared with George."

"I don't know," she said.

"Yeah. Let's do it. It'll be a connection for both of us."

"Well, what if your parents find out? See, this was a thing for the two of us."

"All right. I get it. You want to keep the secret. We can do that. No one else would know."

She frowned. They sat, staring ahead. Annie sighed. Then Sylvia and Sonita came in. Sylvia immediately dropped into the pew in front of the girls and made a bug-eyed announcement.

"Know what we just heard?"

Elspeth raised her eyebrows. "We have no idea, Sylvia."

"I got this call and I didn't want to answer it because we were leaving for the funeral and all but Sonita said it might be important so I did."

"Did?"

"Answer the phone. And it was our aunt and she told me about that guy Travers - you remember that new guy who didn't stay long?" She wasn't really asking. She was telling. "You know, he moved down near Thelma."

"Where's Thelma?"

"South of San Antonio somewhere. Anyway he was killed."

"What!"

"Yeah, like a gang fight or something."

"When?"

"I don't know," she shrugged.

## Arthur

The Mortician seems to have the attitude that relatives of the deceased are too fragile to have contact with the general public. Maybe there is something in the Egyptian

Code of Death Handlers that declares The Bereaved to be unclean. Whatever, I did not react well to being sequestered in a Sunday school room cum holding cell before the funeral. I left the room and marched down the hall, then stopped, realizing I had no place to go. Probably I was trying to escape myself, but a person cannot do that. I opened the door to the sanctuary and saw Annie and Elspeth nodding their heads. Two other girls had their backs to me. I could not be sure who they were. Something one of them said clicked with the others. I did not need to interrupt that so I went back to the Sunday school room to see how Connie was doing.

## Chapter 27: Travers Died

Elspeth asked, "Your aunt called to tell you that?"

"No," said Sonita. "She called to ask what time the funeral started. But while she was talking to Sylvia she mentioned that Travers guy."

"This is pretty suspicious," Sylvia crossed her arms.

"What's suspicious?" Annie wanted to know.

Sonita clamped her hands on her sister's shoulders. "We've got a theory but this is not a good time to talk about it."

"We've got plenty of time," Sylvia objected.

Sonita glared at her. "I'm not talking about quantity. I mean quality. Let's go see who else is here." She grabbed Sylvia's arm and pulled her out of the room.

Annie stared after them. Finally, Elspeth shrugged. "They think there's a conspiracy to kill gays but Sonita feels like it would be rude to bring that up in front of George's little sister."

Annie turned back toward the flower sprays.

"I hope my mother doesn't hear about this," she said.

## Stephen

Looking around at our classmates filling the sanctuary for George's funeral a thought pushed into my brain. What about George and some other dude at school? If George didn't have a girlfriend - although I can't rule Elspeth out of that possibility, did he have a boyfriend? Around here, you can't always tell what's a date and what's not a date. Teens do things in herds sometimes. If herd doesn't work, what about groups or clumps? People pair off within the clumps. A boy and a girl might flirt. Two girls might talk about a boy. Two guys might talk about a hot chick. Maybe two gals might be talking about another girl or two dudes might be flirting. I dunno. It could happen. See, I can't actually say how much George saw Travers Nygren. Who knows why my brother suddenly wanted to go hear some social misfit read poetry. I could make up a story, although I never heard one about George and Travers.

Wow! Oh no. You know there was this time when Travers came to watch George play in a tournament. I wasn't playing but they let me carry George's bag. Some dude from Luling was medalist in the tournament. CHHS did really well - second place team score and George won fourth place individual. Travers had moved off before Christmas without a word to anyone that I knew of and here he shows up at a spring golf tournament. He said guys from his school were playing. We made the turn by the clubhouse and headed for the tenth tee when he just saunters up with this cat-ate-the-canary grin. George gave him a big hug. Are you kidding me! George never hugs anyone. I think it embarrassed both of them. They backed off as if static electricity jolted them apart. They each said about ten words and walked away from each other. Travers didn't follow us through the back nine. There can't have been anything to it because I just didn't like the guy.

Travers Nygren. Tall, handsome, quiet and mysterious. Travers' dad was military. That was why they moved to San Antonio. Apparently every couple of years he started life in a new school. When he showed up the first day of school, he was the buzz of the day. Everyone wanted to know him or know about him. He glided down the hallway and you just knew one coach or the other would be welcoming him to CHHS. That lasted about a week. Travers wasn't interested in sports and seemed afraid of people. A story oozed around that his parents moved here from San Antonio for a reason. His dad was a colonel or a general and his mother had an affair, or Travers stole something, or his mother had a lot of money - the story changed daily. Travers disappeared after class every day like Houdini was jerking his chain. Dan said he was a snob. I thought he was a little older than your typical Caliche Hills senior and that's about the only thought I had on him. George saw him in a couple of classes. In fact, that was the first I knew about him. "Ya see the new guy?" he asked. "Seems nice." That was it up through Thanksgiving.

Travers showed up at church one night to watch our living nativity. Annie played Mary, I was a shepherd, and George back staged the sheep and cow we had commandeered. I watched Travers watch us from the edge of the parking lot. George walked over and spoke to him. They exchanged a few comments and Travers left. Later I asked George, "What's up with the new guy?" If he lived in Caliche Hills for the rest of his life, he would always have been the new guy. George shrugged and told me Travers was interested in theater and just wanted to see how we set up our production.

"He didn't look around that much."

"Said he saw all he needed to see."

After that, I saw George talking to Travers several times at school. One evening George left the dishwashing duties to Annie and me because he had to go to a poetry reading at school. We both turned up our noses. George said that Travers had written an epic poem he wanted to hear.

"We'll be anxious to hear about it," I said in my most sincere and solemn voice.

George glared at me.

The next day Travers interrupted my backswing in Dan's back yard. The three of us - Dan, George, and me, not Travers - were pitching and putting at the mighty putting green we maintained at Dan's place. I leveled off a smooth upstroke and Travers squeaks, "Hey." Then he strides over to

George and musses his hair. "What'd you think, Georgie?" he says. "I write some riveting lines, don't ya think?"

George swung his sand wedge back and forth self-consciously. "Yeah," he said a couple of times. "Good stuff, good poetry. I really liked it."

Dan and I looked at each other as if we just fell onto the yellow brick road. "Georgie?" he mouthed at me. I had to turn away from them. We ran inside for something to drink to calm the coughing fits.

In January, we returned to school from the Christmas break with the same excitement about school that I have toward poetry readings. Along toward the end of the first week, I heard that the new guy wasn't in school. There were fewer stories about why he was gone than there had been about why he had come. Nobody cared that much.

I dunno why I thought about Travers.


## Annie

George disappointed me when he took off with that creep Travers. If the three of us are supposed to have each other's back, then I call it treason to hang with someone like him. All right, I don't know anything specifically wrong with Travers. I just didn't like the way he walked, the way he glided and rolled his shoulders. I could just see him dancing a constant ballet, watching people from the corners of his eyes. He followed football players and checked them out head to toe. Maybe he was going to be a mortician and wanted to be able to gauge a person's coffin size. George only went to a few thespian events featuring Travers. Ten too many, in my book.

## Chapter 28: A Funeral Sermon

Lance set aside his hymnbook. He had selected the hymns for George's funeral so the selection could not explain his inability to sing them. Looking across the congregation, he saw the Thompson family filled the front pew. Close friends supplemented the extended family members for two more rows. What with an overflow crowd in a Sunday school room listening to a contrived sound system, there must be over two hundred people waiting for his eulogy and sermon. What was he going to say?

Lance stood and carried his Bible to the pulpit. The word-processed sermon, finished just two hours earlier lay before him. He knew it was a cobbled mess, patched together from other funeral sermons, selections from a couple of pastoral manuals in his library, and augmented by his knowledge of George and the Thompson family. It was not worthy of this good family and their need but the time had come to speak. He opened the Bible and read to the congregation from the gospel of John chapter eleven, the story of the death of Lazarus. Then he replaced the Bible on the pulpit.

"When we read this story it is quite possible to come away with more questions than answers, in other words, to find ourselves exactly at the funeral of George Thompson.

"Why, when Jesus hears his friend Lazarus is sick, doesn't he go immediately to cure him? Why does he use an obscure metaphor to tell his disciples that he is going to wake his sleeping friend only to have to jar them with the hard fact, 'Lazarus is dead'? Why does he give Martha theology: 'I am the resurrection and the life' but with her sister Mary he breaks down and weeps?

"Or, to turn to the grief of the Thompsons, why did a young man who had so much to offer have to die so young? Why did a good young man have to die so violently and brutally? Why did George enlist in the Navy and thus offer his life for the good of his country but before that becomes even a possibility, he is senselessly murdered - an act that includes no sacrificial gain, no redemptive purpose?

"A few moments ago I read from Psalm ninety, that familiar explanation that a typical life measures seventy years. If we are strong, the Psalmist suggests, we might make it to eighty. He states his point a few verses later as he prays, 'Lord, teach us to number our days.' An excellent insight, even eighty years is not that long. God help us make the best use of seventy or eighty years. Hold on a minute, what would the Psalmist have to say about nineteen rather than eighty years?

"Let's look for help in John's story about Jesus and his friends Lazarus, Martha, and Mary. In the first place, we will never completely understand this biblical story. I am not an old man, a long way from seventy or eighty; nevertheless, I have read this story more than once and studied it some. Scholars can tell us a whole lot about it, but I have never read a good explanation for Jesus weeping when Mary confronts him. Both sisters came to Jesus and said, 'Master, if you had been here, our brother would not have died.' The second time that happened all Jesus could do was cry. When he went to the tomb, John says he was greatly disturbed. Eugene Peterson's version, *The Message*, says that anger welled up inside him. Jesus was angry? Because his friend was dead? Angry at Lazarus for dying, at himself for delaying, at the crowd for gawking at his and the family's grief?

"I can't explain that to you. I can only encourage you in your hurt, confusion, and anger. Consider that God knows right where you are right now.

"George's father tells me that his son's death is not right. I know that. God knows that."


## Connie

At the funeral, I kept looking around. We were sitting on the front pew, which is so weird because we never sit there. The only people I could see were Pastor Lance, the music director, and the choir. I could turn my head a little and see family members, the pallbearers, and a few friends. It would be rude to just turn around and stare but it seemed so out of place for us to be there. And the coffin - right in front of us. Lance talked and talked. I thought he would never quit. Finally, we could stand and look around. So many people. When could we leave? Before the service began, the mortician led us into a Sunday school classroom where Pastor Lance and the coffin were waiting. The coffin was open and there lay George. I wanted to say, "Get up, honey. You have to go join the Navy."

## Chapter 29: A George Story

Lance looked at his congregation and took a breath before continuing. "We will miss George. Among other things, we will not have any future surprises from George. Well, maybe one. Let me surprise you now by telling you how George surprised all of us. Some of you know about the 'miracle of the divan.' There was an old divan in the youth room that needed to be lost. We needed to get rid of it. Arrangements were made to give it away but we could not get it out of the room. I don't know how we got it in there but we couldn't seem to push or pull it through the door. Then one Saturday when some of us came to church to saw it in pieces, we found the divan behind the church. I can tell you now that George did that. I don't know how or who helped him, but I have learned he did it. Cherish your best memories of George.

"After Jesus raised Lazarus, some believed in him and his message. Others plotted his death. You can choose your direction from this place. You can choose to focus on the good memories of the young man we have lost. You can choose to drown in the fog of confusion and the bile of hatred spawned by his senseless death. Life, whatever life remains to each of us, is too short to travel both paths. Lord, teach us to number our days."

Lance waved at four men in the front row who immediately stood and walked onto the platform.

"Our church quartet will conclude the service by singing 'The Irish Blessing.' The final blessing will be a good parting for this service: 'May God hold you in the palm of His hand.' "

Lance walked away from the pulpit conscious of the fact he had read from his Bible but not from his sermon manuscript.

### Annie

I just love Pastor Lance and Willow so that probably made the funeral even more difficult for me. I am the one who told him that George and Dan had worried the youth divan out the back door. I knew it because Alton Granbury told me he had helped them. Nobody knows Alton. He works at Ace hardware and is one of those anonymous middle-aged bland, vanilla people that you never see. Somehow, George roped him into his project and Alton helped them. George and Dan would never tell. No one would ever ask Alton and he doesn't talk to anyone except when you ask him where screws or washers or hammers are, like I asked about mosquito repellent. I told him I was buying it for my brother George and Alton laughed which kinda surprised me because you never expect vanilla people to laugh. So, I asked what was funny and he said he couldn't tell me because George said it was a secret. But I convinced him to tell me.

Anyway, I like it that Pastor Lance told the story and, also, that he didn't say how he knew. I'm sure Dan will never tell his part of the story 'cause that keeps it George's intrigue or gift or whatever. And I'll never tell Dan or anyone that I knew about it. But after Pastor Lance told that story he kinda got caught up in his own feelings. I dunno whether it's best to have the funeral preacher be someone really close or someone who's a complete stranger. You know a complete stranger can read the twenty-third Psalm or whatever and tell you about the need to live a good life since we are all gonna die and there's a heaven waiting. He can tell you the traditional funeral stuff and be calm about it. No, that's not really a good thing. Pastor Lance muddled all over himself but you knew, you just knew that he loved George and he would miss him almost as much as Dad, Mom, Stephen, and I will miss him.

# Chapter 30: Leaving the Funeral

At the funeral Stephen's friend, Tariq, asked how he was holding up. Stephen told him he really didn't know. It seemed as though he had been sleep walking through everything. Tariq said it must be tough having your older brother die and, again, he said he just didn't know.

"I don't believe it," Stephen said.

"Right, man," Tariq answered, "it's unbelievable."

"No," Stephen shook his head, "I mean, I really don't believe George is dead. I keep expecting him to come in the front door saying, 'Boy that run felt good - went a little out of my way it felt so good. Sorry I'm late.' You know, I check his room. I mean, not deliberately go to his room. I just, it's habit, you know. I walk by and check to see if he's there. Or, like I'm out the door and I think, 'Wonder if George wants to go with me?' I'm back inside standing there thinking, 'what's the matter with me? George is dead.' Yeah, I know it, but I don't believe it."

Behind the boys, Elspeth and Annie walked together. "You going to be okay?" Elspeth asked.

"I was just going to say the same thing to you."

"I liked that the quartet sang. I've never heard that Irish song."

"I've heard it before a few times."

"What's that first part mean, about the road rising to meet you?"

Annie waved her hand up in front of her. "Well, if the road rises to meet you, you must be going downhill."

"Oh, I get it. Then it's a prayer that you're going downhill, with the wind nudging your back and the sun on your face."

"Yeah, and a gentle rain on the crops."

"Nice thought."

"Uh-huh," Annie said, "Except, right now I feel like I'm trudging uphill, against a hurricane, in the dark."

"Even so, you could still be in the palm of God's hand."

"I s'pose."

# Stephen

Tariq asked if I wanted to join the pick-up baseball game at the school on Saturday. I said sure. Just another Saturday as though nothing was different. Or, maybe George was off to the Navy or something. That would be different but not a big difference. One of those differences where George would come home and for a while, things would be the same. Of course, not the same because someone has ratcheted up his life to a completely different level and it would never be the same again but it would be a difference you could live with - a difference you could honor. You could say, "Hey, way to go, George." But here George is gone, completely, absolutely. We're having a funeral so we can bury him and I say "Sure, I'll play baseball on Saturday. Life goes on." Just not with George.

The preacher said the usual stuff about all of us seeing George in heaven someday. I know all that. When that happens, that'll be the Grand Difference. It doesn't have anything to do with today or Saturday when I'll be playing baseball like nothing was different.

Elspeth sat with Dan and his family at the funeral. At the cemetery, she came over and talked with me some. She really just looked devastated. She told me Dan and George were her support group. They kept her together and now one major third of her existence just wasn't there anymore.

"How can that be?" she asked. Then she apologized and said, "He was your brother. I don't have any right to become the drama queen here while you're missing your brother."

"It's cool," I told her. "I know you were close to George somehow, in a different way from being a brother or sister. You have your own pain. I know that. You don't owe me an apology."

And she goes, "Maybe it is like a brother - sister thing. I mean, that's kinda how it feels to me. Like - he was a brother to me, you know?"

"Not really," I said. "Could you - I mean, maybe this is too personal, I dunno, but what the heck. If you were like George's sister, then you're my sister too and I can ask you a dumb question, okay?"

"Sure, whatever."

"Okay, so, some people thought maybe you and George were boyfriend and girlfriend, but, turns out, you weren't. You're just friends, right?" She nodded, a questioning look on her face. "Well, follow that thought a little: how is it a healthy high school grad-you-eight, Navy enlistee doesn't have a girlfriend? Not at all. Some people are saying things about why some world-class idiots beat him to death. They're saying a hate crime that goes right to the issue of a nineteen-year-old who's not interested in girls." She started crying and I felt like a world-class idiot all on my own.

"I'm sorry," I said. "Look, I'm glad you were my brother's friend/sister. As far as I'm concerned you fit our family quite well."

"I just can't ..." she said. Without explaining what it was she couldn't, she turned and walked away.

## Chapter 31: The Pastor's Wife

Willow took her husband's arm and walked him to their car. Behind them, the mortician's tent flapped over George's grave. She turned him toward her, cupping his face in her hands.

"He was a beautiful young man and you said wonderful words over him," she said.

He said nothing but hugged her.

"You know," she looked up at him, "the one who comforts is also free to grieve."

"I know that, but thanks for reminding me. I know about grieving and funerals and all that goes with it. I've studied it and lived it. Even if this is just my first pastorate, we have buried several people in Caliche Hills."

She nodded. "A lot of old people here."

"What I don't know anything about is compounded grief, when your child dies and then you learn something new, stuff you never realized about your son."

"Do you think George was homosexual?"

"Never considered it. That's just not something I would have thought about."

Willow looked at the departing cars. "Some people think about it a lot. I know some family members who have to deal with the issue constantly."

"Here, in Caliche Hills?"

"Lance!" She gave him a look. "I'll ask someone I know to check in with Arthur."

"What about?"

"Maybe someone who lives with a gay family member can give the Thompsons some insights."

After a moment he said, "That's not the hardest question."

Willow raised an eyebrow. "What is the hardest question?"

"For me. The hardest question for me."

"Is?" She stretched the word into two syllables.

"Why wasn't I more help for George?"

"Oh, Lance, you are always helpful. You ..."

"Not this time."

"What happened?"

"Nothing. That's the point. Maybe there was something going on with his understanding of himself. I don't know. But I just feel as though I missed something."

"Oh, Lance. You can't help someone when you don't know they need help."

His face fell. She grabbed him in a bear hug. After a moment he said. "Yeah, I guess I do know that. But what my head knows does not match what my heart feels."

## Arthur

We got home somehow. It's funny how I remember certain details at the hospital with crystal clarity, but most of that evening is a fog. The fog has lasted. Well, anyway, we pushed into our new lives. Or maybe the new lives pulled us forward.

George died. Because he was beaten. Or because the doctors killed him, or they let him die, or they did not know what they were doing, or God loved him and took him home, or God wanted to punish me for being a bad father. Or maybe God was busy with war or famine or pestilence. He died. That is all I know for certain.

There was a funeral. Pastor Lance handled it all. Clumsily, I might add. I thought he was distracted. Said some good things about George. The church was stuffed. Never seen so many people in that building. My boss, most of the people out of my office, came. They really seemed to care while we were in our church in Caliche Hills. Back at work, they seem, well, distant.

I like Lance. He is young and energetic and cares about his congregation. He knows Caliche Hills pretty well. That is obvious in the fact that he shows up everywhere. He told a story about George that was news to me. A couple of years ago we all were mystified about the "sleeping couch miracle." There was a divan in the youth room that had been donated by someone decades ago. It had been re-covered a time or two but still grew more grungy, according to the kids, as it deteriorated on the spot. The ministries committee knew that a family on the outskirts of town would love to have it. Working on the premise that one church's trash might be a poor family's treasure, we agreed it would not be a bad idea to let them have it. It was time to re-do the youth room with some new furniture anyway. However, the sticker was that we could not get the couch out of the youth room. It was as if we built the room around it. In fact, although I do not remember if this is true, it could be that one of our building renovations put a door where there once was a larger opening. I suggested that but no one agreed with me. Anyway there we were. Of course, we could have chopped the wretched couch into pieces and removing it would be a matter of trash-bagging it out the door. But we had promised to give it away. Several people were in favor of pooling our pocket change and we could buy them something - at the very least a used sleeping divan from a thrift store. Lance and the ministry committee were stubborn about it. They said we needed to move it sometime and only as a last resort we would buy something. This conversation took place one weekend. The following Saturday several of us showed up with saws, hatchets, and whatnot to destroy the monster only to find the couch sitting outside the back door. Lance told the funeral congregation that George had come up with a solution. He and two friends had managed a miracle. Lance had guessed as much but George had insisted that no one tell who did it. It was a surprise to our whole family. Later I asked Stephen if he were one of the "friends." He swore that this was the first he knew of it. He assumed, with the rest of us that George was just as mystified by the whole thing as we were.

It was a good story and I could tell by the reaction that no one had a clue George had pulled off the "miracle." Still, at several points, Lance tried to say something about the senseless manner of George's death and he could not complete his thought. Of course he was - is - emotionally involved, but I thought maybe it was something else.

## Chapter 32: Home with Help

Two unfamiliar SUVs guarded the curb in front of the Thompson house after the funeral. Marie and a couple of aproned churchwomen welcomed the Thompsons to their own home. An aroma of chicken potpie that would lift even the darkest spirits wafted from the kitchen. Sylvester and Dan came in to eat with the family. Connie had invited Elspeth to join them. The churchwomen played hostess or waitress insisting that Marie sit at the table. She refused, feeling she should stay in the kitchen. Arthur wanted everyone to get a plate and find a place but they would not have it that way. Annie said they needed George to organize the meal and Stephen laughed. There was an awkward half-a-second until Arthur laughed and everyone chuckled politely. That was not too hard to do. Marie reminded everyone of a Beef Wellington that George had fixed. "You wouldn't believe the delicate crust," she said. "And the beef was not too bad, although a little rare."

"Bloody awful," Sylvester corrected, "is what you said when we got home." That was a little amusing.

"Remember the time he climbed into the belfry?" said Annie.

"He got locked in," Arthur said.

"What?" Several people did not know this story.

One of the churchwomen wanted to know how he got up there. Arthur explained about the rungs in the wall in a back hall. Someone else wanted to know who locked him in.

"No one. He did it himself," Arthur said. "You get up there by pushing up a trap door. The secret is you have to latch the door open. He did not know that. It just fell shut. It was not so much locked as simply shut. There are no handholds or knobs. He couldn't get it back up."

"How old was he?"

"Nine or ten."

"Nine," Connie nodded.

"Who found him? How did he get out?"

"He took care of that," Arthur laughed. "You know we usually walk to and from church. It was not too unusual for him to be playing with Dan and catch up with us about the time we got home. When he was not home and did not show up for a few minutes, I walked back to check on him. I found him trying to find a place to jump off the roof. I went inside and brought out a ladder, climbed up and led him down."

"What was his excuse for climbing into the belfry?"

"Same as always. It needed to be done."

The belfry story reminded Arthur that Sylvester had taken George and Dan back to the church and directed them as they installed a couple of knobs on the trapdoor. "You get a Yea-Boo for that," he scolded his friend. Sylvester wanted to know why and Arthur explained he was happy for him to put the boys to work doing something that needed doing but, in reality, he was only encouraging them to climb up there again. They probably did, but since the knobs were in place, no one ever caught them doing it. That little bit of low-level carpentry led to George's interest in Sylvester's garage woodworking shop. "A memory in soft lights," Arthur said. "I liked it."

By the time the banana pudding had disappeared, George scampered again through every part of their lives.

"Why did he join the Navy?" Now there was a question. Connie grinned, waved her hand as if she had a story there. She coughed, covered her mouth with her napkin, and turned deer-in-the-headlights eyes to her husband.

"He wanted the training," Arthur answered.

"You know that makes sense," someone said.

"Sure," another voice. "He had such a solid head on his shoulders. It would have been good experience plus they still pay your way to college, don't they?"

"I thought that had run out." A general disagreement ensued and we began clearing the table.

When Arthur arrived home after his first day of work following the funeral he passed one of the same churchwomen leaving the house. The next evening Marie met him at the door. "Just leaving," she said. Two nights later Connie told her husband he had missed Francisca Dominguez by scant minutes.

With all those arms around them, the Thompsons felt less isolated in their grief.

## Annie

So many people bringing us food. I guess food, preparing and eating it, is family for us. Mom taught George how to make enchiladas. That was Thanksgiving for our family. We "turkeyed out" at other family meals, so we preferred enchiladas at our own Thanksgiving dinner. Mom knew a special cheese sauce. A family secret. "Families can have secrets but there are no secrets within the family." That was her tag for the enchiladas. Every November, George and Mom made enchiladas and we heard, "Families can have secrets but there are no secrets within the family."

## Chapter 33: A Baseball Game

On Saturday, Stephen had the lawn to mow and decided that was a good excuse not to play baseball. Stephen liked sports, especially golf, but not particularly baseball. George had told him that swinging a baseball bat was similar to swinging a golf club but not the same. In fact, they were enough different that playing baseball could mess up your golf game. Stephen never was completely convinced but on the other hand, George always seemed to know what he was talking about. With the lawn finished early, though, Stephen changed his mind and wandered over to the school lugging his fielder's glove.

Tariq was there as were the Grainger brothers. On the field were several dudes who usually populated these pick-up games. One fellow Stephen could not place. He looked familiar but somehow Stephen just could not pull an ID out of the back of his head. Nobody ever introduces themselves at these games. Either a player knows everyone there or he is not willing to admit he does not know somebody. When Stephen arrived, they were playing a pop-up game. One of the Graingers was hitting fly balls. The first person who caught five would come replace the hitter. When Tariq saw Stephen he shouted, "Hey, Stevie makes ten; that's even, let's choose up." Stephen hated being called Stevie.

He also hated being chosen last but that did not happen. Most of the time someone chose him in the middle of the selection process. As he would explain, "I'm a golfer, not a fielder or hitter, but I'm an athlete so I can play any sport well enough." The unknown player was chosen last on the other team. Canfield waved him to join his team saying, "All right, Tom. You're with us." It hit Stephen. He was Thunder-Tom from George's old scout troop. Incredible! He remembered Thunder-Tom as big, menacing, and evil. Stephen reasoned he, himself, must have grown some. Tom, in the meantime, had put on some weight and gotten ugly. You would not call him fat, a little chunky perhaps. Well, well, well. A demon from the past just got exposed as a fraud.

# Stephen

People might think we are all carbon copies of one another. Dad, Sylvester, Dan, George, and I play golf. We have for several years. Some set of us - a threesome, foursome, or occasionally a fivesome - play a round of golf every week, every season, in all kinds of weather. George led our high school team. Dan made the team the last two years. I got on the team this last year mostly because the coach figured George's little brother ought to have something to contribute. Once George showed up for a match dressed like Payne Stewart in knickers and bright red and yellow socks. Fortunately, CHHS was the home team because coach sent him home to change.

Far as I know, George is the only guy in Caliche Hills who can cook. That is, a young dude. I know some older ones who cook. Both our dads do outdoor bar-be-que stuff. One time we had Dan's family over and George - he was fourteen at the time I think - he fixed beef Wellington. I had never heard of it. He takes this piece of meat, some kind of beef, and wraps it in pastry and then bakes it all day. I guess it's kind of like a baked Alaska. No, that's not right. Well, anyway, how do you know when it is done? If you have a steak on a grill, you can tell how it's coming. You can even cut in to it and see if the meat is rare, medium, or well done. Now with this beef Wellington thing, you can tell if the pastry looks cooked or whatever but you have no clue about the beef. I guess you have to know what you are doing or trust the recipe or something. How was it? It was great! Even Annie ate it and she is one picky eater.

Growing up behind George and Annie I just followed in their wake. George is a perfectionist who always did things right the first time. Annie is just the opposite. If it works, fine. She doesn't care if the corners are rough. Well, she has a little perfectionism in her. She can be very fussy about colors and textures. We are all competitive. The family loves games and we bike together. Dad, George, and I have played golf ever since I can remember. George spent more time choosing the right shirt and pants or cleaning his clubs than I spent practicing driving or putting - and that was a lot. Plus, he talked more about my performance than about his own. He was protective of his little brother but no more so than I was protective of him.

He was a Boy Scout briefly. That summer his troop scheduled a camp out in the nearby state park. Dad signed up to go as one of the parent sponsors and he asked permission for me to tag along. The three of us were excited about the adventure, George planned to work toward earning several merit badges, Dad made noises about being in the wild with his boys, and I was giddy over the idea of spending the night in a tent. At the last minute, Dad had to bail out on us. His job in Austin with Dell Computers scuttled family plans occasionally. He works with quality control and, as he would say, "If we get some low quality bouncing around town, I'm the one who has to go control it."

I helped George set up our tent. Dad had bought us a good tent with a built-in bottom and great snap-together aluminum tubes that set-up quickly. Then George rolled out his sleeping bag and placed a small box just inside the tent where he arranged his toothbrush and toothpaste. An older boy walked over to see our tent. He wore faded jeans and an old scout shirt sporting several badges and a rumpled scarf around his neck.

George had on a new scout shirt, regulation walking shorts and knee-high socks. Mom had ironed the whole uniform including the scarf around his neck. The older scout, his name was Thomas, we called him Thunder-Tom, looked at George and then at his "vanity shelf" and started laughing. For the next hour or so, as the camp was taking shape I felt like all the other boys were playing some sort of pass-the-secret game and George was the butt of the game. The scoutmaster and the fathers fed us a lunch of pot boiled stew and then announced a scavenger game designed to work on several merit badges.

The scoutmaster assigned some of the older scouts to mark a trail; others would then be given instructions and have to follow the trail with the goal of returning to the camp within an allotted time. One of the more senior boys, Thunder-Tom as it turns out had the task of administering the exercise. That meant, among other things, that he prepared the instructions and assigned George his trail.

While the first set of scouts was out trail blazing, George and the second set of boys listened to the scoutmaster go over the reading of compass azimuths and various signs they could expect to see on the trail. Rocks could be stacked in a certain way or branches bent to show the direction to follow. There were signs to indicate caution or danger. We learned we would have a compass and written directions. The fathers marked off ten yards and had the boys pace that distance so they would know how many of their own steps would match that distance. For my part, I badgered several of the fathers until I finally got someone to agree that I could go with George when his turn came.

After the trail-setters returned, Thunder-Tom explained that there were four different routes to follow. Somebody gave the trail-followers a compass and one of four different lists of instructions. The trails led in four different directions from the camp but eventually they would cross one another and all would return to camp past the scoutmaster's tent. Four boys (plus one little brother) waited to receive their instructions. The boys then set off in five-minute intervals.

George and I had to wait until last. Our instructions directed us to walk along a fence by the side of the road leading into the camp. We were to look for a double forked tree and then turn ninety degrees to the left. I took off at a run. The road ran alongside parkland covered with mesquite and live oak trees. Most of the timber was seriously scrubby and barely fifteen or twenty feet high. There were vines and bushes making rather dense undergrowth but showing well-traveled paths through the area. I had to stop for my meticulous brother who read and reread his instructions. "Come on," I urged him. "Let's find that double forked tree."

He looked up with an odd grin on his face. "What's a double forked tree?"

"I dunno. A tree with two trunks I guess."

"Wouldn't that be just a forked tree?"

"Well, c'mon. We'll know it when we see it."

"I'll bet Thunder-Tom wrote these instructions. Pyracantha is misspelled. The directions are garbled in a couple of places and, in fact, they don't really make sense."

"So? Let's just walk in a big circle and head back to camp."

"Can't quite to do that. There are a couple of places I have to make notes. I have to write what I see. And then, for instance, I have to

194

find a spot and sight a compass reading on a pyracantha bush. So we can't just walk around for a while and then head back."

At the time, Thunder-Tom's addled directions didn't bother us. We found the double-forked tree and I made sure to point out that the tree forked into two large trunks at its base and both of those trunks forked again, making it a double forked tree. We turned left. Not long after our turn, we thought we heard two scouts talking but we never saw them. Later we passed a family, a mom and dad with two elementary age girls, hiking through the park. George stopped me abruptly and motioned for silence. He then pointed to a doe and yearling ahead of us. Amazingly, they didn't seem to be aware that we were walking up on them. At least for a few seconds they weren't aware, and then they bounded off, gliding effortlessly over sumac bushes. We found George's spot and the pyracantha bush. George determined that the bush was precisely 102 degrees from our spot making it sort of east southeast of us. I showed George Yaupon Holly, Live Oak trees, Mountain Laurel and redbuds and dogwoods. He was surprised that I knew about such things. He asked what else caught my attention. I was looking for mountain lion and bear tracks. He told me there was very little chance of lion and none of bear but that didn't dampen my enthusiasm. I loved the hike until we had to climb a hill. We were following a path that branched. A sign pointing left told us the trail would return to the camping area. Pointing right a sign told us we would find the river there. However, the directions gave us a compass reading telling us to forge ahead for a quarter of a mile. In front of us was a rock cliff going up about twelve to fifteen feet. Above that was a ledge and then a hill sloped away from us that was - who knows? It was a hill. I could not see how we were going to get up on the ledge in the first place.

"Are we going to have to go up that?" I asked.

George was just looking up at the hill. "That's what it says."

"And then what? Maybe we can walk around this and get back on our trail."

He pointed at the instructions. "No we have to go a quarter mile this direction and look ninety degrees right and write down what we see."

I turned to my right and announced that if I were a quarter mile higher I would probably see a river. "Let's go this way, back to the camp."

George shook his head and grinned. "No, this is going to make a lot of points for me."

"What merit badge has to do with climbing rocks?" I wanted to know.

He put his hand on my shoulder and flashed the biggest smile. "Stephen this has nothing to do with scouts. This is about Thunder-Tom and me. He has given me a challenge none of the other boys will have. I'm going to go back to camp and tell him what I can see at the top of that hill."

"Why would he do that George?"

"Oh, who knows?" George began walking back and forth, inspecting the rocks before us.

"That doesn't make sense," I insisted. "Not that I expect him to make sense, but the scout fathers wouldn't let him do something like that."

"I don't imagine they know. Look, this is kind of a crevice that shouldn't be too hard to climb." George stuffed instructions and compass into his pockets and experimented with handholds and steps and then stepped back down and looked at me.

"I'll tell you what Stephen. Why don't you head back to camp up that road? It's not very far."

"No, I want to go on with you."

"No, hey, you know what?" George began waving his hands in the air. "Tell them we got separated and you think I'm lost."

I didn't want any part of that and told George so. He agreed that it would not be right to pull such a prank on everyone else. I pointed out that Thunder-Tom was pulling a prank on him. George just shrugged and told me to head back to camp. I said I was following him.

Actually, climbing the rock cliff was a piece of cake. It wasn't that high and we found easy access to the ledge. Both our hands were roughed up some and George's knees showed some scrapes (fortunately for me, I was wearing jeans and a t-shirt) but we felt ourselves conquering heroes. It turned out that the gentle sloping hill was the larger challenge. Scrub brush covered the side of the hill. No hiking trails revealed themselves to us. The brush tore our clothing and scratched faces, arms, and legs. We continually had to check landmarks. Unfortunately, there were no good landmarks. The whole hillside looked about the same. George kept pulling out his compass and pushing it, along with seeds, leaves, and bits of bush trash into his pocket. We really were separated. Some of the time, we couldn't see each other but we never got to where we were out of earshot. Both of us yelled and complained almost every step of the way. At some point, I had decided it wasn't fun anymore. Finally, George yelled at me to find my way toward him. He thought we were at the top of the hill. When I got to the place where I last heard his voice I found him sitting on a large rock. "Is this about a quarter mile up?"

"Who knows? But this is about the top of this hill. I think it begins to go down some from here."

I stepped up on the rock and looked around. Scrub brush and mesquite surrounded us. Our outer perimeter was a ring of hills that looked very much like the hill where we were. "What are we looking for?" I wanted to know.

"Beats me," he said. Pointing across his compass, he waved at the broad side of a nearby hill. "I don't see anything particularly distinctive over there. But you know," he turned toward me, "it might have been easier to tell if we had gotten here sooner." He was right about that. The sun was behind some clouds just on the edge of the hills. We had spent most of the afternoon on our hike.

We decided we needed to get back to camp the best way we could and forget about Thunder-Tom's directions. The instructions would have led us further along the line we had followed up the hill. George didn't think that would help us much. We finally decided to go back down the way we had come. Backtracking through the shrubbery was no easier but we did come down the hill a little faster than we had gone up it. Once we got back on the park pathway, we ran into two scouts sent out to find us.

Back in camp, the fathers were quite agitated about our lateness and our appearance. We were covered with scratches, our clothing looked like we had climbed through barbed wire fences and we both could build bird nests with the twigs in our hair and our socks. The fathers brought out first-aid kits and supervised the doctoring of our cuts. The scoutmaster discovered immediately that George had bogus directions. George never complained but the scoutmaster scoped it out. Maybe he did the wise thing in not confronting Thunder-Tom in front of the boys. I did, however, hear him tell Tom's father that they needed to talk. In the meantime, Thunder-Tom and two other scouts found reasons to duck their heads and cover snorts and laughter. Most of the boys just thought it was bad luck and wanted to get on with supper.

That night in our sleeping bags, I asked George what this meant. He told me we had run into a bully and not to worry about it. "Stephen," he told me, "this is no big deal. We'll tell mom and dad the good parts and leave out the rest." And that's what we did. But it was not lost on me that George never returned to scouts.

## Chapter 34: The Fight

Stephen's team took the field first. They spread out with Tariq pitching and guys in place as first baseman, third baseman, right and left fielders. The batting team provided the catcher. With five in the field rather than the official nine, players had to cover a lot of ground. Tariq pitched for the high school team, so placing fielders did not matter much. Most of the boys cannot hit his stuff and the few who can - well, if someone really tagged a Tariq pitch, the rest of the players would not be able to get to the ball, so they were just out here for fun. Tariq went easy on them resulting in three fly-outs. If he wanted to, he could have had three strikeouts.

On the other hand, since Tariq was the ONLY pitcher among the ten boys, when his team batted they scored five runs. Stephen even hit a triple - a great shot right through the seam between everybody on the left and everybody on the right. After two innings with his side up by twelve runs, they reshuffled the lineups. This time Stephen had to face Tariq and that looked a lot different. However, they discovered, much to the pleasure of the four boys on his team, that Willie Grainger, the younger of the two, could occasionally throw a strike. For the third game (the second game lasted three innings with Tariq's team winning eight to three), it was decided Tariq and Willie would remain the pitchers. The other eight players changed places. For the first time Thunder-Tom and Stephen were teammates.

After holding their opponents to a one-run start, they huddled around home plate to determine the batting order. Tom and Stephen found themselves in the last two positions, so that gave Stephen a chance to remind Tom they knew each other from scouting days.

"You remember George and Stephen Thompson from a scout camp-out a couple years ago?" Stephen asked.

"Nope," he said as he watched Willie Grainger swing wildly at Tariq's first pitch.

"You made up a map that got us lost."

He turned and frowned at Stephen for a moment. Then his face flickered and he began a smile. "Oh yeah," he crowed, "your brother's the faggot who prissied up his tent."

Stephen hit him square in the nose. He growled and rammed his head into Tom's large target of a stomach. Tom stumbled backwards and both boys rolled around in the dirt. There was so much dirt flying the other boys could not tell who was Stephen and who wasn't. Players pulled them apart. Three boys were holding Stephen and four had some part of Tom. Tariq stood with his finger in Tom's face. Stephen yelled at him, "George was always a better man than you Thunder-Tom!"

"Nobody calls me that!" he yelled back. Much as he tried to break free, he could not wrench himself from their grasp. Blood was all over his face and he was crying and blubbering. "Thunder Tom?" someone said. "I had problems with gas," he cried. "I couldn't help it."

The three holding Stephen released their grip and moved toward Tom. All the boys were talking at the same time. "Did you call George Thompson ..." "You're crying because Stephen called you ..."

Stephen picked up his glove and started for home. After two blocks he started laughing and laughed all the way home. But, when he came in the front door he was sobbing so hard he thought his ribs would break. Connie came running from the kitchen all upset asking what had happened. He looked a sight, dirt and blood all over him, and crying as if he had fallen out of the swing on the playground. When Stephen saw the distress on his mother's face, he sobered up quickly.

She led him into the kitchen, sat him at the table, and washed his face with a wet dishtowel. Stephen told her what had happened and that led to some quiet tears of her own. "I was afraid they had come back for you."

"They?"

"The ones who killed George," she cried.

That evening Connie told Arthur about the baseball experience. He wanted to know what had happened. Stephen tried to blow it off. No big deal, Stephen shrugged, just a misunderstanding. Arthur was not buying.

"No really, Dad, it wasn't anything."

"Your mother thought it was something. Why don't you let me in on it?"

"Well, there was some lard-bucket there who had been on a scout camp with the two of us only he didn't remember us at first. When I tweaked his memory he called George a name."

"What kind of name?"

"Ugly."

"Okay. What specifically?"

"Dad ..."

"All right. You do not need to tell me what you are not comfortable saying. Still, I would like to know what happened. It will not hurt you to tell. Might help."

"Well this guy is a real loser. He played a practical joke on us and at the game today he called George a faggot."

"And then what? He started a fight with you because you're George's brother?"

"Uh, well Dad, you see calling George a name sort of started the fight."

"I see. He calls your brother a name and you shoved him and things went on from there."

"Oh we, uh, rolled around on the ground some and the guys broke us up, but, uh, I didn't shove him."

"He shoved you?"

206

"No, Dad. I punched him in the nose."

"You did?" Arthur's eyes grew large at this point.

"Yes sir. Blood all over the place."

"That could be a serious injury. Broken nose or worse."

"I don't think so. I tackled him and knocked him down and we wrestled some. I think I dented his pride more than anything else."

"Hmmm," he said. "And what about when you came home. Your mother thought you had been hurt. Outside of wrestling with you what else did he do to you? He didn't hit you back?"

"No. It was pretty much a one-punch fight, really." Stephen looked away and laughed. "A very one-sided fight. I, well, he was pretty embarrassed and I laughed about it all the way home and then, for some reason ..." and, at that point, Stephen broke out crying again. Arthur stood and pulled his son into his arms. Stephen was thinking he was too old for that. He must have been mistaken.

# Annie

Life goes on I guess. I mean, I have to eat
and sleep and whatever because I cannot not
live. Mom would say that, you just can't not
do it - whatever it is that you have to do. So
we eat breakfast and do things and eat lunch
and do more and eat supper and go to bed.
Dad goes to work and Mom goes over to her
shop or somewhere and Stephen does
whatever guys do.

Gwennie pushed and pulled on me until I
went to the Barton Creek mall in Austin with
her to hang out and we ran into Sylvia and
Sonita who were hoping to run into a couple
of guys and they were all, "Do you think
they're here? Where could they be?" Like
maybe, they would just die if they never saw
a hunky boy. They didn't stick with us long
because they thought I made a scene. I
mean, running into some lame dude who
isn't really going to pay that much attention
to you anyway is not the most important
thing in the world. And I told them so. I
wasn't yelling. I was just firm.

But Gwennie didn't bail on me. She never
would. We got cherry mint chocolate chip,
just one dip in a cup because the cones are
so sugary, and sat in the food court,

watching girls looking for boys and boys looking for trouble.

"What's it like?" Gwennie asked me. "What's it really like?"

"I dunno how to say it. You know?" I told her. "There's just no way to talk about it. I mean, it's like the sun goes down and the next morning it isn't there. And you just know that the sun has to come up, but it doesn't and every day you're thinking it has to come back. But it doesn't. It hurts so bad, but you know it can't go on like this, but it does."

Stephen and I just subconsciously or something fell into dividing George's chores. Stephen already mowed and edged the yard. He picked the job of carrying out the trash and I'm not sure what else. My jobs were dusting and vacuuming, and I added bathroom cleaning and kitchen duties George had done. No one asked or offered. We just did it. Neither one of us chose the occasional cooking George did.

One evening I pulled dishes, silverware, and stuff from the dishwasher and began to put it away. I realized we had been "helped" by a number of volunteers who brought in food like a fabulous spinach casserole and an utterly uneatable pecan pie - I mean how hard is it to put together and bake a pecan pie? And they cleaned up after meals and put things away where they should go if they were in their own homes. Sometimes I got the feeling they thought they were correcting our mistakes in arrangement. Anyway, I began pulling silverware out of drawers and dishes from cabinets and placing them back in proper order, stacked or arranged according to matching sets - not all plates on the left, all saucers here and cups there. No! All the matching plates and saucers and cups and whatever together, smallest on the top. And the silverware lined up not just dumped. When I finally got it all back where it was supposed to be I held my arms out and said, "There! How's that?"

Nobody answered.

## Chapter 35: A Talk with the Pastor

Arthur stuck his head inside the door of the pastor's study. "Hey, Lance," he said. "Got a minute?" Lance waved him in and pointed to the chair in front of his desk.

"So, what's up, Art?"

Arthur settled himself, looked around the room for a moment, and then turned his attention to Lance. "Well," he started and then looked down to pull at his pants leg. "I'm afraid that ..." He looked up. "You know, you really did a fine job at George's funeral."

Lance smiled and waved a hand. "No, I didn't but thanks for saying so. I miss George, too, you know."

"Yeah. Yeah, I know that." A pause. "Lance I want to apologize for coming at you so strong at the hospital. I do not believe any of this crap about George might have been gay. I hurt and maybe I tried to find someone to blame ..."

The pastor waved both hands. "Forget it, Art. You were obviously stressed. You should be very angry about your son's death." He looked at the father carefully. "You still are, aren't you?"

Arthur looked away. "Oh, you bet, I am angry. But I'm also frustrated and confused."

"Why wouldn't you be?" asked Lance. "What happened? I never got a straight story about how he died."

"He was hurt worse than they knew. They fixed what they could and were prepared to transport him to Austin if his injuries were beyond what they could handle." Arthur sighed. "It was not a matter of what they could handle. His injuries were beyond what they could diagnose."

Lance raised his eyebrows. "Malpractice?"

Arthur shrugged. "Probably not. I am more angry about the scum that beat him than at the men who tried to save him." He looked away. "Too many questions. Too much grief. I do not want to take on that one right now."

He looked back at the pastor, "Mind if I tell you a couple of stories? Have you got some time?"

Lance opened both hands and leaned back.

# Arthur

What stories to tell? I wanted to open up to Lance. But with what?

Several days - or maybe a week - after the funeral Syl and I plowed through a rocky philosophical field, a minefield in my way of thinking. I asked him what sort of father must I be who did not even know about my own son's struggle with his sexual identity?

"He wasn't struggling with anything about himself," said Syl. "He was pretty comfortable with himself. Other people made assumptions and they struggled with their own assumptions."

"Assumptions?"

"Yeah. George never told anyone he was gay. He just, well he just was not convincingly non-gay. To some people, that is."

"Wasn't convincingly ... what in the world are you talking about, Syl?"

"Art, what I mean is, he never dated. You know, Dan told me there had been a few girls who tried to get his attention and he was simply polite to them. Seemed oblivious to their interest in him. He just never returned the interest."

"What about Elspeth? I mean I know they were not boyfriend/girlfriend. But wouldn't it appear to someone that they might be?"

"Apparently not. I have no idea what goes through teen-age minds, but apparently not. But that is only one piece of the puzzle here. George was always neat, clean, and orderly."

"And those are not male heterosexual traits?"

"Probably not in today's youth culture."

"Okay, maybe this makes sense. Maybe some people saw him as cut from different cloth. How come he and I never talked about this? How come - I do not know - why was I not more plugged in to his life? We did not play golf as much the last couple of years because he was playing with the team or he had school projects or he - well, Syl, he was in your workshop a lot lately. That is a good thing. I did not feel like I was neglecting my kid."

"You weren't. You're a good father, Art."

"My son is dead. That does not make me feel a good anything, particularly not a good father."

"Yeah, I know. And that will stay with you a while. But at some point I hope you come around to the reality that some other son-of-a-bitch did this and not you. It's not your fault and there is not a thing that you could have done to change it."

It was not like Sylvester to use that kind of language but, somehow, that was one of the most helpful things anyone said to me.

About that time I asked Dr. Sauerwein if he knew what caused homosexuality and whether there were any way to determine who was or wasn't a homosexual. His immediate response was that he did not have a clue. He had studied about it, though not much, and it was not something that had ever come up in his practice. But, he had a few minutes to spare and was willing to hear what I thought about it.

I told him I did not know what to think. I was asking him what he thought about it.

For a man who did not have a clue, he went on for several minutes about genetic development, family and social influences, and experiences with positive and negative role models, and I cannot remember what else. His conclusion, however, and this got my attention, none of that really mattered. It was all beside the point.

"What are you saying, Doc? What is the point?"

"Finding some guru who knows how we are made is really beside the point," he said. "The more important point is how you feel about George and his death."

"What I really want to know is, was my son a homosexual?"

Doc leaned over his desk and asked me, "What difference does it make?"

"It makes a lot of difference!" I said.

"No, Art, it does not."

"How can it not matter, Doc? It matters!"

"In the first place, it does not matter because we can never know the answer to your question. You are wasting time, energy, emotion - you are wasting your life - pursuing a question that you cannot answer. Secondly, whatever George's sexual orientation, he never acted on it. From what I know and from what you have told me it appears that he did not have a girlfriend or a boyfriend. Moreover, in the third place, George was a sterling example of what any parent wants a child to be. He exhibited character. He was …" At that point the doctor found himself unable to continue.

Maybe Doc's silence meant more than his lecture.

What really threw me was the day help came looking for me. I had just turned into our driveway when an SUV pulled up to the curb. Big honkin' Toyota Sequoia from which stepped a small woman, black hair, pale skin, jeans, and chambray shirt. She looked familiar but I could not be sure. As soon as she said my name, the familiar nasal voice told me I knew her but still could not remember why.

"You don't remember me," she said.

"Well, yes, I know we have met but I can't place where."

"I'm Wanda Friezen. My husband is your dentist."

"Oh sure. You act as the office manager for Richard."

"That's right."

I was mildly surprised to see her but even more surprised about why she had come visiting. Of course, I invited her inside and discovered, pretty much as I had expected that I was the first one home. We sat in our great room where, much to my satisfaction, she came straight to the point. She offered condolences for George's death and then told me she was an active member of PFLAG."

"Flag," I said, "I've never heard of it."

"I'm not surprised," she answered. "P - F - L - A - G. It stands for Parents and Friends of Lesbians and Gays. After a conversation I had with Willow Carroll, I thought you and Connie might like to know about the Austin chapter."

My mouth went dry and the hair stood up on the back of my neck. "Why do you suppose we would be interested in any chapter of PFLAG?"

"We understand that George was a victim of gay-bashing."

"That's a leading theory about the crime." I guess I bit off my statement.

"This, I know, is very presumptuous of me. I'm not here to suggest anything about George and you would not be prepared to accept anything along that line anyway." As I raised my eyebrows she added, "Nor should you be."

I cleared my throat. She continued, "I simply would like for you to know that there are, oh, a few families living in Caliche Hills who are members of PFLAG. We might have some insights and experience that would be valuable for you."

"Do you know something about my son that I don't?"

"Only that Dick has filled some of his teeth. Absolutely nothing else. Honestly Mr. Thompson I am only here to offer a source of, that is, a community of care and comfort."

"That's very kind of you," I said in what sounded to me like a cold and unkind voice.

She left quickly after that. As I watched her drive away I remembered she and Richard had been at the funeral.

The congregation had filled the church at George's funeral. Connie and I are well known in town as well as in Austin to some extent. It was not surprising that our friends and acquaintances were there. But youth came in large numbers. I did not think George had that many friends. Probably most of the young people there were friends of Annie and Stephen, yet I was certain that a good many of those kids were recent graduates of Caliche Hills High. They were from George's graduating class. I asked my two about it and they said I was right;

George did not have all that many close friends. However, most of the school knew who he was and respected his character. That was good to hear.

Driving home one afternoon, I forgot my turn. Daydreaming I guess. Happens a lot lately. I drove to the next large parking lot and turned in so I could head back toward home when I realized I had put myself in front of the Constable's office. Aleta Diaz was walking toward her car.

She smiled and said, "Hey, Mr. Thompson," as I jumped out of my car.

"Any news about my boy's attackers?"

"Get right to the point, don't you?" She offered her hand to shake.

I shook her hand and stepped back rubbing my forehead. "George's murder is always at the back of my mind. I cannot say I think a lot about who did it. But I sure burn up a lot of energy around why they did it."

"We can answer why better than who, Mr. Thompson. Although there are multiple layers to the why question and our answers are superficial at best."

I looked around for a moment. "What answers do you have?"

"Only the barest layer of why. Someone hates gays and took it out on your son."

"And you come to that conclusion because?"

"The only real evidence anyone has found is the word spray painted on a fence near where George's body was found."

"Is it possible someone painted that word earlier? That it had nothing to do with George?"

"Possible." She smiled briefly, and then frowned. Neither of us said anything. I turned to go.

"Mr. Thompson."

I turned back. "Yes."

She looked down at the pavement and then back at me. "I know you must think we are terribly incompetent if all we have is what anyone could see. But I want you to know," She stepped toward me. "This is the number one thing Smitty and I are working on."

The number one thing. I wish George had been the number one thing I was working on at some point. For some time now, I have been excruciatingly conscious of my job. I mean, I have been focused on keeping my job and - I do not know - out-of-body conscious of my job. We talk some, you know, in the halls, out in the parking lot, about jobs disappearing to India or wherever. So, you have to focus on your job. Of course, none of us in quality control will see our positions yanked overseas. But what if someone in a related department loses a job and one of us gets lateraled to that department. It could happen. So, on the one hand I've got my attention on staying gainfully employed and, on the other hand, I am very aware that I am very aware of keeping my job. I mean, how much have I neglected my family? Yet, is it really neglect if I want to continue to be able to provide for them?

This probably does not make a bit of sense but I have really beaten myself up about it.

Sylvester recently asked me if I knew why suddenly homosexuality was so bad. I figured being queer had always either been morally bad or indifferent. He said, "No, this was new."

"Whadda ya mean new?"

"Well," he said, "in the last several years it has become the one really bad bugaboo."

"That makes no sense." I mean, sometimes he can be so off the wall.

"Sure it does. And you know why?"

"Yes, I know precisely the answer to your obscure little puzzle. But," I poked him in the chest, "I'll just let you explain it to me."

"The collapse of Soviet communism. That's why."

I just snorted. I was changing sparkplugs when he showed up and gave me an excuse to take a break and sit in the shade. Connie had brought out two glasses and a pitcher of lemonade.

"Does that explain global warming too?"

"Listen, Art, I'm serious. Fundamentalist Christians no longer have atheistic, godless, Russian communism to worry about."

"Oh, fundamentalists. I see."

"Yeah. And they have to sub-render their racist and anti-Semitic opinions."

"Sub-render?"

"Sub-something. They have to hide their biases."

"I'm not so sure they do. But that could be a good thing."

"So then Gays are the only large scale obvious evil out there. And that is only because the Religious Right needs a grand enemy."

I looked up at the sky. "God revealed this in a dream, I suppose."

"Actually, I read it in a book."

"That erases all my skepticism."

"No, this is from a responsible researcher and author."

"And I would recognize this author/researcher?"

"I doubt it. I can't remember who wrote it."

"But you wanted me to know about this theory."

"Yeah, sure. Well, it seemed important yesterday."

Syl asked how well the car ran so we shuffled back to the garage. I cranked the engine smiling at the gentle purr affirming my superior mechanical skills.

He closed the hood for me with a flourish and gave me a thumbs up.

Sitting on the hood, he rubbed his chin. "Know something," he mused.

"What?"

"The word homosexual is not in the Bible."

"Sure it is," I countered.

"No. It is not. The word homosexual is a fairly recent invention."

What difference does a word make, I thought. "Paul definitely says something about lying with the same sex. He calls it unnatural."

"Yeah," he scratched his head. "That is pretty clear." However, admitting that did not slow Syl any. "He had some strong biases didn't he?"

"Paul? I don't think so. He was the number one missionary to the Gentiles and he called Peter on the carpet for his biases."

"Well, yeah, but he got cross-ways with Barnabas over his nephew Mark's immaturity."

"That's hardly a bias."

"Yes, it is. I just said so."

"Excuse me."

"And he set back women's rights over two millennia with his 'keep quiet' charge."

I laughed. "In two thousand years, no woman has ever paid attention to Paul. How can you say he set back anything? Have you ever met a silent woman?"

"Sure. She was also deaf."

"I'll bet her hands were moving constantly."

## Chapter 36: Pastoral Advice

After a long consideration, Arthur told Lance only about Sylvester's breakdown-of-Communism theory and his take on the Apostle Paul's influence on women, leaving off other stories he had planned to mention.

"So, there you go," Arthur finished, "A silent deaf woman but her hands were all in a flurry." Lance looked quite non-committal as if he did not find it amusing. "Oh," said Arthur, "I forgot you have a deaf cousin."

"Yeah, Art, I have pretty much heard all the deaf jokes. Was there another story?"

Arthur looked away. "Maybe another time," he said.

Then, feeling a need to change the subject, he asked why Episcopalians ordain gay ministers. "That seems to show some Christians read the Bible without finding a condemnation of homosexuality."

Lance nodded and murmured, "Presbyterians are also talking about some changes like that."

"I didn't know that. Since when?"

"Not anyone in this Presbytery. We don't make changes quickly or easily."

Arthur shrugged. "So? Is your definition of proper biblical interpretation, 'This is how we've always done it'?" He made that cutesy "quotes" signal with his fingers.

"To be honest with you, Art, a couple of ministers have tried to recruit me to back an effort to recognize gay ministers."

"I would guess, from what you have said so far, you refused to go along with them."

Lance adjusted his chair. "Not so much refused. I just haven't responded. I'm pretty busy learning how to be pastor/preacher/administrator. I do not see myself as … uh, I dunno …"

"A rabble rouser?"

"I wouldn't put it like that."

After an awkward pause, Lance renewed the conversation. "Well, back to the Church of England," he looked up at the ceiling. "Frankly, I have no idea why Episcopalians do what they do. They did give us the King James Bible. Nevertheless what they do in their churches doesn't carry a lot of weight with me." Lance leaned forward in his chair. "Arthur, I need your help."

"You need my help?" Lance nodded. "This is a first. What about? Whatever it is, you've got it."

Lance sat back. "I need your patience with me. I haven't found my, uh, well, let's say I haven't found my sea legs yet on the whole homosexual question."

Arthur rubbed his chin. "I can appreciate that."

"A professor told our class once that the best preparation for ministry was experience."

Arthur interrupted him with, "Isn't there a joke - something about you can't get a job without experience and you can't get experience without a job?"

"I don't know about a joke, but that's where I am. I have never, to my knowledge, dealt with a gay in any way. I completely missed anything George might have told me or asked me. I deeply regret that."

The two men settled into a deep silence for several minutes.

"To follow up on your sea legs analogy," Arthur spoke quietly. "we are in the same boat, so let's try to row together. Okay? Now, how about a serious question? How did you find out about the couch miracle?"

Lance grinned and waggled a finger in Arthur's face.

"Pastor/parishioner privilege, my friend. No can tell."

"It's a good thing I like you," Arthur responded.

## Annie

Anyway, I got a summer job with Dr. Tangelo the Vet. Doc T always is after me to work there because he is just so sure that I would make a great veterinarian, which is totally bogus even though I love dogs and cats, it's just not what I want to do. But working for Doc T during summers is cool and doesn't mean I have to do it, like, forever or anything. You would think that since I did this last year and he so wanted me back that this was a no-brainer. But, I dunno, I just wasn't sure that I wanted to leave Mom at home all by herself. Not that she's that much all by herself. You know, with Marie coming over, and church people in and out, and what with her spending some part of almost every day at her shop. And, yes, she did offer to have me work in the shop this summer, like she offered last summer, but we both knew that wasn't a serious invitation. I mean, OK, I am an artist in that I make jewelry and stuff, but I'm not an art major, so I would be the only one in the shop who didn't actually meet the requirements and that would mean I got a special pass. I didn't want it. On the other hand, I did think about it for two whole minutes this time before I turned Mom down. She was practically in the other room like she already had heard me say "No" before I said it.

So, why was I remembering this? Oh yeah, Matricia, the office manager and animal nurse for Doc T got all serious my first morning at work wanting to know how I was doing. She's real nice but not so much a personable person. She's all about dogs and cats and not so much people. I thought it was an effort, a genuine, sincere effort, but still, you know, work for her to ask me about how we were taking George's death. Later, she brought it up again and wanted to know what I thought about who did it and why? I didn't know. I haven't heard anyone say anything intelligent about who might have beaten George or why they killed him. There can't be an intelligent answer to those questions so how could any of us guess. Or, even more important, in my humble opinion – IMHO in texting code, why would we want to talk about it?

"Why don't you want to know who did it?" Gwennie and I were swimming at the Muellers and she was hassling me. We had been swimming, that is. We were sunbathing, you know, on towel sheets on the lawn next to the pool.

"Why should I want to know who they were? They couldn't be anybody from Caliche Hills, so I don't want to know who they were."

"But you want them caught and punished, don't you."

"Sure," I turned on my back. "What did you do with the lotion?"

"You had it last."

"No, I didn't. Oh, wait. Here it is."

"You just have to want them in jail for life. For the rest of their lives."

"Yeah, but I don't need to know who they are." Honestly, why do people have to tell you what you want or feel?

Last summer George dropped by the vet's to bring me my retainer that I am supposed to wear way more than I do, but it makes me look all geeky and I don't like it. I intend to wear it two hours a day but for some reason it's easy for me to forget it. Anyway, he was sorta hanging with me before he went to lose a bunch of golf balls when Matricia goes on about her "funny" cousin. I go "funny how?" She goes, "Like, you know, gay." George got this weird expression on his face. "How did she know he was gay?" he wanted to know. She goes, "He's forty-five and out of the closet."

"What happened when he came out?" George asks.

"I dunno. I wasn't there. They live in Georgia."

"But what happened when you and your family heard about it?"

Matricia looked out the window and rapped her pencil on the desk. "Not much. We already figured he was that way. It wasn't any big surprise really."

"So you're okay with that?"

"Sure, as long as he stays in Georgia. I never much liked him. He's a sissy and thought he was too good for any Texan relatives." She snickered. "As long as he's a long distance relative, he's easy to make the butt of our jokes."

Funny how that story just changed in my mind. Last summer George was showing interest in my friend Matricia. Sounds different today.

We have a "funny" cousin, too. He lives in Nebraska and we never see any of his family. To be honest, I don't think I've ever seen any of them except his dad, my some-kinda-uncle. He isn't Mom or Dad's brother. They always refer to them as aunt, uncle and cousin but they are way more distant. He was through here one year, which led to some stories about growing up with uncle whosis leading on to how old is their son and how long has it been questions. Dad said he is way old enough to be married and have kids and Mom goes, "Married?" and laughs. "Well, yeah," goes Dad, and Mom does a limp-wristed thing while she walks into the kitchen. "Oh," says Dad. "I forgot." They did not come to the funeral. I'm not sure my folks even let them know.

# Chapter 37: A Conversation One Evening

Summer reached the critical mass of windless, humid heat at the very moment that the youth group of the church participated in a Habitat for Humanity project. Stephen's thumb throbbed a brilliant shade of purple. Annie's sunburn radiated a cry for help. She left early with Gwennie for a lotion bath. Stephen stayed around to help clean up. Lance had promised a ride and that explains why the two of them were the last to leave the yet-to-be-completed house. With the last tools dropped into the trunk of Lance's car, they fell into the front seats.

Lance started the car, revved up the air-conditioner and looked at Stephen who had reclined his seat and appeared to be asleep already. "How's it going?" was his simple question. Stephen opened his eyes and looked at the sun visor. Then he began to talk.

"This summer I am working at the Caliche Hills public golf course," he said. "This is my second summer working at the course, so I no longer am low man on the totem pole. Mr. Weathers, the manager of the course, has always been interested in our golf game. He's a PGA teaching pro so anything he said to George or to me was special. He taught me to putt like Gary Player: keep your head down and listen for the ball to hit the bottom of the cup. I had a real problem of looking where the ball was going before I even hit it. Mr. Weathers gave me a couple of days off for the funeral and all. I really appreciated that but I was glad to get back in the clubhouse after two days. It was pretty dreary at the house. At least I thought so. When I came in, he put me to pulling golf carts out of the cart shack and lining them up ready to go in front of the clubhouse. When I still had a couple of carts to go he told me to run the course and reset the tee boxes. Most of our tee boxes cover about fifteen yards, front to back. The tee markers could be placed anywhere in the box. Once a week we moved them forward or backward. The groundskeeper repositions the holes on the greens. Mr. Weathers wouldn't let anyone else do that. But he would have one of us "kids" - that's what Mr. Weathers calls the students who work the course - one of us 'kids' would reset the tee boxes. The minute I walked in from that job he said, 'Thompson run the gobbler on the range.' The course owns a small tractor-like vehicle with a worm sort of device that picks up golf balls and throws them in a cage on the back. For obvious reasons we call it 'the gobbler.' I went to the john first and then headed for the cart shack to start up the gobbler. The whole day was like that. He never let me stop. I didn't have one minute to think. When I got home I sure was tired, but it was a good tired."

Lance murmured an "I'm listening" sound.

Stephen continued as if he had not noticed. "No one was using the driving range while I drove the gobbler but I remembered one time last year when I had an earnest driver on the range. George worked the course too, last year. Most days we worked half a day and played golf the other half. Is this the coolest job or what? Sometimes we worked and played the same schedule; others one of us worked while the other golfed. I was driving the gobbler that day and George elected to hit a bucket of balls. He aimed every ball in the bucket at me. Now that's not as dangerous as it sounds. The gobbler operator sits in a protective cage. Even so, you flinch when a ball hits the cage. Golfers supposedly have an advantage over other sports in that neither the ball nor the hole moves unlike a pitched baseball or a wide receiver running out for a pass. George figured if he could hit a moving target at one-fifty to two hundred yards, then pitching a ball onto a stationary green would be a piece of cake. He actually hit the gobbler several times and was close quite often. I yelled at him every time. I told him a four iron was no match for my tank and I was coming after him. We both laughed about it all. George was fun.

"I guess I did have some time to think. Mr. Weathers had me doing a lot of physical jobs. He certainly kept me busy, but I didn't spend any time, not much any way, talking to people. No interaction with the golfers."

"Good," nodded Lance.

"Do I believe George was gay?" Lance looked at Stephen briefly. "Uh-oh, that question again. You know, we have to consider it. I guess until now I never thought about it. In the last several months, a year maybe, I was conscious of what other people said about George or even to him. But that was always their problem. Not his. George was just George. He was busy. He was focused. He would get around to girls or romance or sex whenever he thought it necessary. George had his own agenda, his own priorities. That does not make him gay. Or, I realized while driving the gobbler, I guess it doesn't make him hetero either. It just doesn't matter. Well, anyway, that's about where I left it."

Good night, thought Lance. It is not ten miles to Stephen's home. What a lot to say!

The pastor turned off the engine in front of the Thompson's house. "You know, don't you, that you can come see me any time?"

Stephen pulled himself out of the car, shut the door, waved, and said, "Thanks for the ride."

Lance watched him disappear into the house.

"Any time," he mumbled.

## Arthur

I am worried about Connie. OK, we are all a little wacky, grieving, angry, confused. George did not just die; somebody killed him. He did not just die violently; death changed him, recreated into someone we did not know. It is hard to know how to grieve over the loss of your son when you really aren't sure who the son was who you lost. "Whom" you lost. Well, at least I know George well enough to know he would have corrected me. None of us is handling this well. But Connie has her own little spin on George's death. She said something the other day about the dangers of Naval Intelligence.

"Naval Intelligence?" I said. "What are you talking about? We don't know anything about Naval Intelligence." It startled her. She seemed to have been in her own private hiding place and I surprised her.

"You know," she spluttered. "In the Navy." She lurched out of the room.

One evening we were watching the news, some story about a terrorist suicide bomber. She made a muffled noise, a gasping cry. "Not again," she said.

"Yeah, it's constant," I said. She dabbed her eyes and I realized she had started to cry a little.

"Hey, Connie," I tried to pull her toward me but she resisted.

"You think they're half-way around the world." She was pointing at the television. "Then they show up here." She had a full-scale cry going now.

"What are you talking about, Connie? Do you think ...?"

"Oh, Art! Don't pretend you don't know," she sobbed.

I had no idea what to do. I have no idea what to think.

Not that I can handle my grief any better. I am not ready to rewrite George's history while I flounder around trying to figure out just what his history was. Russell Skinner asked me the other day - Russell works with me in Austin - he asked, "Wouldn't you like to find those bastards and beat their brains in?" I told him, "No, I never want to see them. But if I did I would want to know just what they had against George and who did they think he was while they were beating his brains in." I yelled the last part and apparently scared Russell. He apologized for his question. I apologized for yelling and then told him that maybe it helped me realize that I really would like to beat them silly.

I do not remember ever yelling at anyone before, but now I have done it several times since George's death.

Connie does not sleep well. One or two nightmares a week. So? I am having a difficult time sleeping, too. But I think she lives her nightmares. Francisca Dominguez called to ask me how we were doing and then asked how I felt my bride was doing. I told her we definitely were not on a honeymoon. "Isn't that the truth!" she responded. Turns out, she had seen Connie at the grocery store acting a little funny. She thought it was a little weird. What did Connie do, I wanted to know. Francisca could not describe anything specific. Connie kept looking around in an unusual way. She walked over to Connie to express concern. As she approached, Connie stared past her and put her hand to her mouth. Francisca turned around but did not see anything that should have disturbed her. They had a brief disjointed conversation.

"I'm only calling because I'm, well, concerned about her. Is there anything I can do?"

No, I assured her, there is nothing. There is no way to bring George back and there is nothing anyone can do to fix whatever is wrong with us. I wish there were.

Last night Connie asked me who our congressman was. Wendell Slover, for crying out loud. We put a sign in our yard and bumper stickers on the cars. We do not really know him personally. But anyway. The reason she asked, she told me, was she wanted to write him a letter. Okay, fine with me. What would the letter say?

"I don't want you to try to stop me," she said quite firmly.

"Why would I want to stop you? Write your letter. I'm just curious."

"Maybe I'll just call his office."

"Okay."

"To get some information."

"Sounds like a plan."

"I need to find out who it is in the military hierarchy who makes assignments."

"Of course they don't make assignments until a person has joined the military and gone through their initial basic training."

"Oh right. That's understood. But the government does so many things secretly.

We never know what they are doing behind our backs."

"Unfortunately, I guess you are right, Connie. Nevertheless, George would not have gone through boot camp without us knowing it. That's not possible."

She was quiet for a long time. I could not tell what she was thinking. I had been reading a Ludlum novel so everything she said certainly meshed with my train of thought at the time. She had a Maeve Binchy story open on her lap. It did not seem likely that anything she had read stirred up a Naval Intelligence plot.

As she left to get ready for bed she mumbled, "You don't know everything, Art."

She had me there.

Probably I merit the title sadistic devil but it seemed like a good idea at the time, still does. Earlier I had told Connie we should take a drive, check on some houses. She dropped her book on the lamp table, pushed both hands against her knees, and struggled out of the chair. Did I have to carry her? First, we head for the door. Then she has to go into the bedroom for sunglasses. Next, we are back to the door and she wants a straw hat. Penny notices the movement and lets us know she loves to ride. I tell her no, not this time. Connie comes back in the room and calls her to go with us. Well, why not? Now we are outside the door but Connie trundles over to the mailbox, had not checked the mail yet. Bills and circulars. Only, she would rather not take them with us, so back inside. Finally in the car but she complains she does not care about new construction. Does not matter, I tell her. It will be good for us to get out of the house. Of course, we do not even get out of the neighborhood before she is pointing left and right. Look what they have done! What is going on there! Penny jumped in the back seat and went to sleep.

People can hide in Caliche Hills. Most of us never intend to hide, but the trees and hills bless us with camouflage. Driving along a two-lane road a visitor would have no idea that a dozen homes lay over the hill to the left and an entire community hides around a corner. We enjoy scouting areas that we have recently neglected. That is what we did. After a bit Connie was suggesting places she wanted to see - additions to homes, new sun porches, a gazebo, hardiplank siding, about a million dollars of remodeling loans around the edges of Caliche Hills.

"There's not much to see along this road," she noted.

"No. Seldom much traffic on this road. The guys like to run along here. They do not have to dodge the pickups and they can avoid the fumes."

"That's nice."

She leaned back against the headrest, a low tune rumbled in her throat.

"What're we stopping here for Art? You can't see much from here. Let's go up around there so we can look over the valley."

"Sure. But first I want you to see this."

She sat up.

We looked at cedar, live oaks and a weed covered pullout area by the side of the road. The scrub trees prevented us seeing much in any direction. Ahead, across the road from us, vultures pulled at a deer carcass.

"Okay. What?"

"This is where they found George, hon," I pointed through the windshield.

Hammers in the distance woodpeckered someone's renovation. Along with revving pickups climbing a nearby hill they reminded us we were not alone. We sat on the backside of nowhere, visually shrouded from any hint of civilization. Not more than a quarter mile around the corner waited a convenience store with gas pumps and a car wash. But a person would not go there from here or come here from there. This was an "oh, I forgot about that road" route only suitable for running without carbon monoxide or for brutalizing someone without spectators.

"The killers painted insulting graffiti on the fence there. Thank God someone has painted over it."

She pulled her hand quickly to her mouth. After a moment, a soft "Oh" escaped her. We sat for maybe half a minute longer then I pulled back onto the road.

"We don't ever have to come back here, Connie, but I just felt we needed to do this."

I drove straight home. She never said a word until she brought up her letter-writing project.

## Chapter 38: Tee Box Duty

Dan has an awkward, almost Arnold Palmer, swing but he sure can hit the ball far. Dan met Stephen after his morning tour of duty at the golf course for an afternoon eighteen. Stephen watched him drive the green on the number four par four. Of course, it's a short par four but nobody tries to drive the green because you have to hit over trees, uphill on a dogleg left. Dan just stepped up and pulled a draw that appeared to be right into the middle of the green. It made Stephen's six-iron lay-up to the hundred-yard marker look wimpy.

"I've never seen you go for the green here before," Stephen protested.

"Fourth hole, third lost tee. What am I doing?"

"Skunking me. That's what you're doing."

The boys holstered their weapons, mounted their golf scabbards on shoulders, and tromped over to Stephen's pitiful lay-up.

"We don't have George along counseling us on course management; telling us to play smart," Dan noted

The green was thirty feet above their heads. Stephen could barely see the flag.

"So how much did you ever follow George's advice?" asked Stephen.

"Not that much."

Stephen swung his pitching wedge and the ball disappeared somewhere on the green.

When the boys got up to the green Stephen's ball was fifteen feet from the cup. Dan's ball lay in the fringe just off the back of the green.

"Too much club," Stephen laughed.

He birdied the hole. Dan had to settle for par.

"Don't knock course management," Stephen needled.

Coming back down the hill, they saw four guys walking off the third green toward the fourth tee box.

"San Antonio tournament," said Stephen.

"Yeah," Dan agreed. "They're from someplace west of here."

"You're thinking Boerne."

"No. Boerne wasn't in that tournament."

They crossed a small creek and walked toward the fifth tee box. Thompson hit first since he had the honors. While Dan set up, Stephen watched the four dudes hit their tee shots. Three of the four lost their balls out of bounds in the woods left of the fairway.

After Dan hit, Stephen said, "Those dudes razzed George. They didn't like him."

Dan looked at him. "Did you have tee box duty today?"

Stephen smiled. "Yeah. I'm still on duty."

Dan grabbed one marker and his partner grabbed the other and walked as far back as they could go and still consider ourselves within a tee box for the fifth hole. That pretty well defined their day: hit a drive, move the tee markers. The culprits didn't just move them backward. They moved them left or right, or where they could, off the box when it looked like there might be some legitimate repairing of the turf. Their twosome played quicker than the four following them meaning they never had a chance to see what Dan and Stephen were doing. Of course, they were making things difficult for anyone else following the foursome. Never thought about it at the time, they would have said.

Sitting in the clubhouse drinking cherry seven-ups, they watched the four out-of-towners trudge by toward a car. Shaking their heads they muttered, "worst game" and "didn't remember this course being so tough."

"Stephen, that is downright funny."

"Best golf game I've played in a long time. By the way, who won?"

Dan laughed. "We did."

Both boys laughed hard.

Dan sat up, leaned forward propping his elbows on the table. "Okay, they were rude to George and we punished them with a practical joke. I had fun."

"Yeah. So did I."

"What if we knew they were the ones who killed your brother?"

"We don't know that. They wouldn't be stupid enough to drive over here and play golf."

"I know, I know. I'm just sayin'. What if we knew who did it? Three or four dudes we happen to run into and we know they did it."

Stephen glared at the window. "Now you're ruining our fun."

"I'm sorry. It was too much fun to mess up like that. But I can't help but wonder what I would do."

"Get away as fast as I could," Stephen said. "That's what I'd do."

"Yeah. Me too." He sucked on his straw. "Moving tee boxes is about my limit on revenge."


## Dan

Stephen explained to me that the heat must have gotten to him. Sometimes I can't believe the Texas heat. Steam rises off the asphalt cart paths and the brown grass where the sprinklers don't reach crunches under my feet. Usually Hill Country Texans get heat and humidity together. When Stephen plays golf he can ignore the Texas steam bath much easier, but driving carts to member's cars and jogging back to the clubhouse breaks out a sweat bath in a hurry. Any chance he got, he ducked into the clubhouse to chill out, literally. He told me when he was inside, the metro section of the San Antonio Express-News caught his eye. "Lead in Death of Caliche Hills Youth." The headline told the whole story. One paragraph reminded the reader of George's death followed by the simple statement the police had a lead and a reference to the south side of San Antonio. In other words, the reporter didn't know much. Stephen threw the paper down but then picked it up again. There was only one high school in south San Antonio who ever competed against CHHS. It just possibly could be that Stephen knew who killed George. He yelled at Mr. Weathers that he had to go and headed for home.

I got a call at the checkout counter at Ace Hardware. Stephen practically yelled into the phone that he had found George's killer. After he called, I told my boss I had an emergency. Forty minutes after Stephen had seen the article we were "boogin' it" down 281 for San Antonio.

"How do you know he'll be working at La Cantera?" I asked him.

Stephen looked at me. "He did last year and he met George and me at the car with a cart just after school was out for the summer."

"How did that go?"

"What?"

"When he saw who you were."

"Oh, he made a crack about us needing the practice."

We didn't talk much until I turned on the loop around San Antonio.

"How we going to handle this?"

Stephen shook his head. After a bit he said, "I'm thinking major confrontation. He did it or he knows who."

"And if we're sure he did?"

"I'm sure. Yeah, I'm sure. We'll hold on - forcefully - we'll hold on 'til the cops come."

I love the golf course. La Cantera hosts the Texas Open. One elevated tee overlooks the whole city of San Antonio - a fantastic view, but it makes it hard to concentrate on your tee shot. Stephen reminded me about chasing Tiger Woods all over the course this year. But we weren't thinking PGA tour or any golf at all when we pulled into the parking lot. I parked and waved off the cart boy. Wrong kid.

We crusaders strode toward the practice range. He had to be there. But he wasn't. Stephen told me he knew where the cart garage was. Maybe we could find him there. There were a few guys busying around the place but not the one we sought. I told him I would ask inside and see if he might be caddying for someone. Who knows, he could even have been playing. About that time, though, the culprit himself came around the clubhouse.

"Hey," he grinned. "Look at this. Pretend golfers from Caliche Hills. Here for a lesson?" Then Stephen stepped around from behind me.

Our culprit's face rearranged itself into a somber expression. "You're George Thompson's brother aren't you?" He stepped toward Stephen and reached for his hand. The movement startled my friend. Stephen absently lifted his arm.

"Man, I am so sorry about your brother. He was a class act. One of the best we ever faced."

"Uh, you're sorry?" Stephen mumbled. I was surprised.

"Yeah. Our whole team was shocked. We were glad he graduated, of course, but nobody deserves ... well, you know." He looked from me to Stephen. "You guys here to play golf?"

I'm sure my mouth would have made a practice-putting cup.

"No," Stephen said. "Just bummin' around."

The only thing I said on the ride home was, "What were you thinking?"

Stephen didn't answer.

## Chapter 39: What's Up With Him?

Annie had the refrigerator door open long enough that she wasn't sure whether she was looking for a snack or just enjoying the coolness. She decided on drinking a peach Fresca when she heard the front door open followed by some stamping and then another door slammed.

"Break a hundred?" she yelled and chuckled to herself as she popped open the can.

### Stephen

I can see that George might have been gay. I'm not ready to say that out loud. I never will. But just playing games in my mind I can go, "What if ..." Honestly, I would really have problems with that. Who's to say what's reality and what's prejudice? It is not something where I can feel comfortable. The truth is, I mean the real hard nut, the truth is - what does that mean about me? If George could be gay, and like I said that doesn't go down easy, am I gay? Really! Could this be a genetic thing? What are the odds, if one sibling turns out homosexual, wouldn't that be something in the family bloodlines? I heard Dad talking about this with someone just the other day. There's this nature/nurture argument. There is not the least doubt in my mind that George did not choose to be a homosexual. I have a bag full of questions and confusion but not about that. George never woke up one day and said, this is how it's going to play out: I'm gay. Never happened. So, what are we left with? If George was one (big if, remember), it had to be something he was born with. I've got the same DNA package from Mom and Dad that they gave George. Okay, I'm going to think this through to the end and then I'll erase all these thoughts and never come here again. I like girls. When I go hang with friends, I talk to girls. I go to school dances and dance with girls. I'm going to ask someone, a girl, for a date - this summer. I will. I have never thought about another guy in, you know, that way. All right. We're done here.

Man, it's hot. I'm heading for the Mueller's pool.

## Chapter 40: Nightmares

It is very early in the morning as Connie enters through those magic doors that know you are coming and whisper themselves out of your way. No one sits behind the information desk. An older woman with time on her hands and neighbors in her heart will "man" the desk about eight this morning, but not yet. Connie moves quickly down the hall knowing exactly where to find the intensive care unit. You would think one or more nurses would staff the ICU even if it is too early for doctors to be in the building but no one is here either. Nobody, that is, except for the patient.

Connie touches his arm and his eyes drowsily attempt to focus on her face. "Mom," he mumbles, "I'm really thirsty."

She brushes her hand along his cheek and then finds a glass of water with one of those bendable straws. She holds it before his face and he begins to suck just a few drops into his mouth. A smile is beginning to form but then he gasps. Suddenly several alarms go off. Devices at his head, on the other side of the bed, and two on the wall over her shoulder are hee-hawing at her. People in white flood the room. A man rudely pushes Connie aside and she falls into the corner.

"We're losing him!" someone yells.

"Crash cart! Crash cart!"

"Code blue, this is a code blue."

A police officer elbows next to the bed and shakes his head. "Code red."

Four men in naval uniforms rush into the room and grab the patient's body. They run with him from the room trailing an IV pole that hangs horizontally against the doorframe and then crashes to the floor.

Connie yells at top of her voice, "WHAA, WHAA, WHAA!"

She wakes in a cold sweat. Her nightgown wads around her body. Her left wrist hurts because she punched the pillow. Arthur props up on an elbow starring at his wife.

In the bathroom, washing her face, she begins to cry. She hugs herself rocking and moaning, "whaa, whaa, whaa." Arthur steps behind her pulling her into his hug.

"What were you saying?" he asks.

"It's a question, I think."

"What's the question?"

"It's an empty question. I don't even know how to fill it with intelligent words."

## Connie

As anyone can imagine, I really do not like to sleep much. I'm having a little trouble distinguishing dreams from reality. I can't say for sure that I know what is real and what is not. My children have learned from me that there is no sense worrying about tomorrow. Our imagination makes up nightmares that always are worse than what really happens to us. They are so convinced of this because I believe it passionately. That makes me a good salesperson. I believe to the core what I teach my children. Now, it turns out their mother is wrong. Worse than my imagination is the hard reality. I just do not know.

Yesterday (or some other day before today), I was cleaning vegetables and dividing groceries between the refrigerator and the freezer when I heard men whispering. I recognized something like "-gence." Maybe the full word was intelligence. And I heard hissing words that might have been "spy" and "suspect." I actually went into the back yard to see who was there but they had gone or had hidden cleverly so I could not see them.

When I came back into the kitchen, Annie was pouring my tea. She asked what I was doing outside. I didn't want to upset her so I made something up about fresh air.

Oh yeah, that was the grocery store day. Maybe someone followed me home from the store. As I was selecting a cart by the front door of the market, I waved at a friend who nodded toward me and said something to a man about "lost her son." I didn't know him. He was wearing khaki pants and a short haircut. Inside the store, I thought I caught a glimpse of him in the next aisle talking quietly to someone. I couldn't see the other person. As I turned into another aisle, the stock boy looked at me and then quickly ran to the back of the store. As he went through the double doors into the storage area at the back, he passed the man who had to be a Naval intelligence officer.

When I got to the checkout counter, Ensley, the checkout girl was laughing at something Mrs. - oh, the woman from Welcome Wagon

- I can't think of her name. Anyway, they had a conversation of some kind going until I got there. Then they shut down completely. The Welcome Wagon lady didn't even speak to me. Ensley gave me a cheery "Find everything?" like she had nothing to hide.

## Chapter 41: Calling

"Caliche Hills Sheriff's office." Such a bright, professional, optimistic voice told the caller simply by answering the phone she, or someone to whom she may connect her, can solve her problem. But Connie knew better. They never had. Still it was her job to call them to accountability. She asked for Aleta Diaz.

"No, I'm sorry, Mrs. Thompson" Aleta responded. "Like I told you yesterday, we haven't learned anything new."

It's a script. Connie could have written it or could recite it with her. Nothing new.

"Would you like for me to visit you, Mrs. Thompson?"

"I'm sorry?" Connie said. Now that is different.

"I'd be glad to come by after my shift. If that would be helpful. I don't mind."

How sweet. A smile creased her face. "That is so sweet of you officer Diaz. No. I don't think so, but thanks for offering."

"I have got to talk to Art about encouraging Smitty to ask her for a date," she thought as she replaced the phone on the kitchen counter.

## Connie

We live in a beautiful neighborhood surrounded by oak trees and various bushes that alternate a variety of colors of flowers. Redbud trees tell us summer is on the way and cactus blooms during the summer. I am walking downhill from the house when I notice two or three blocks ahead of me a beach. I turn to look behind to make sure that I am in my home neighborhood and sure enough there's our house and behind it the mountains point to the sky, fresh snow at the top inviting skiers. Someone running past me jostles me. I recognize George. He's wearing running shoes, a white sailor's uniform and one of those cute navy white sailor's caps. Another runner knocks me aside. There are four, maybe five of them. They wear black ninja outfits and masks. George is in trouble. I push grocery carts at the men and then throw a gardening trowel. There's a pitchfork around here somewhere.

I know I saw one this week sometime. I run toward the storage shed - somehow I am back in our backyard. Where is it? I have to find it to save George. I cannot find anything I need! Suddenly Art holds me and rubs my back.

"It's okay. It's okay," he coos.

"No it's not," I sob. "It's not. It's not."

## Chapter 42: Sedatives?

Doctor Saurwein shook his head. "You could have mentioned this earlier," he said.

Arthur shrugged his shoulders. "Well, I felt it was just a matter of needing rest but these nightmares are disturbing her sleep ... my sleep."

Both men laughed.

"Connie gets my sympathy. Not you."

"Okay. I can do without your sympathy. But how about a sedative for Connie?"

The doctor turned in his chair, rubbed his head and then steepled his fingers. "How about you bring her in and I'll give her a prescription?"

"Or you could give me the prescription. Uh, wouldn't it be simpler, now that I am here …"

Doc interrupted him, "Whatever happened to respect for my profession?"

Arthur snorted.

Saurwein leaned forward. "Art, bring her in."

## Annie

I read this great story about Adoniram and Ann Judson who were missionaries to Burma and for a time they separated because their work took them to different places but they planned to think about each other. What they would do is they would go outside and look at the full moon knowing that the other one was also outside looking at the moon. That was just so awesome. I think it's a great love story although that's not what the author intended. I mean, that wasn't his main purpose. Anyway, I really enjoyed the story. I hate it, though, when I read a book I like but can't find another book by the same author. Someone left this old book at the church. Since no one claimed it, I borrowed it and then returned it after I read it.

I like to read. In fact that's the main thing I do indoors during the summer. Harry Potter is for kids and *The Lord of the Rings* is for guys. I prefer love stories but not sex stuff which Stephen and I started calling carnal science fiction because - well, that just seems to fit. Right now, I am rereading Madeleine L'Engle's *A Wrinkle in Time*.

That's the first book I read every summer, ever since - well, okay, last year was the first time I read it. But that's what I'm doing and will do in future summers. Last summer I just cocooned in my room all summer and read unless I was swimming with Gwennie or hanging out somewhere with friends. It has been harder to stay with the book this year. I hear mother walking around and every so often I just have to go check on her.

The other day I heard the teapot whistling so I wandered into the kitchen. Mom never leaves the teapot on the stove long enough for it to whistle like that. She had a cup with a tea bag set out and it looked good so I pulled down another cup and poured water in both cups. I put the teabag in her cup until the water turned a deep auburn color and moved the bag to my cup. I was just throwing the bag in the trash under the kitchen sink when Mom came in from the back yard. She had, I dunno, a kinda funny far-off look in her eyes. She picked up her teacup, gave me a silly half-smile, and leaned back against the counter. Maybe five minutes later I finished my tea, put the cup in the dishwasher, and went back to my room. Neither of us said a word.

## Chapter 43: The FBI

The FBI maintains a San Antonio office. Stephen helped his mother find the phone number off the web. In fact, he said, the San Antonio FBI can be contacted through their own web page.

"Why in the world would any sane adult want to talk business or crime on the Internet?" Connie wanted to know. "That's fine for George because he loves to use the computer but not for me." Did she say George? She meant Stephen. It was a waste of time, though. The lady who answered the phone didn't even hand her off to a special agent of some kind. Connie told her it was important for her to talk to someone about the conspiracy leading to her son's death and she cut Connie off. Oh, she was polite about it but Connie knew she wasn't getting past this watchdog. A local sheriff, constable, or police chief has to call in the FBI, Mrs. Thompson was told. She could not demand an investigation as a simple private citizen.

## Connie

I told Willow, our nurse/pastor's wife, how much trouble I was having getting the FBI involved. She is so sweet. The whole time I'm talking to her those big brown eyes never leave my face. "Oh my," she says. "Oh, Connie, I am so sorry." Of course she hasn't got a practical idea bouncing around anywhere in her pretty little head. I was not looking for advice, it's just, every now and then you enjoy talking to a listener. I will give that to Willow she soaked in each word as if she was sucking the venom right out of my heart. Maybe that is not so impractical after all. I sure felt better when I finished my story.

## Chapter 44: The Media

One of the TV stations out of San Antonio features an investigative reporter who loves to get in the faces of public officials. He's the one Connie wanted. Surprisingly she got to talk to him. The phone number on the screen directly connected to him. For a minute or so he was very interested but when she gave him George's name he said he knew all about that case. He was sure the station handled it well and there was nothing he could do to help. Click. That was it. He hung up without a by-your-leave or thank-you-ma'am. From now on, the Thompsons would be watching a different channel.

## Connie

You drop on your knees and scrub if you want to get the kitchen floor clean - Mama Teresa standards clean. Over the years, I have come to understand what all goes with that. Old, torn, faded jeans; high school booster club, ripped tee shirt; head scarf; rubber gloves; sweat in all the old familiar places; and the door-bell rings - the perfect summer ensemble. Leaving only the gloves behind, I waddled to the front door and found Aleta Diaz.

"May I come in?" A soft beige summer top and pants, this was the first time I had seen her out of uniform.

"Has Smitty seen this outfit?" The words were out of my mouth before I thought. She gave me a blank look and said she thought so.

We settled in the great room. She refused lemonade at first until I assured her I needed one. Then she wanted to know how I was doing.

"Fine, just fine." I gestured at my clothes. "Doing a little cleaning."

"I don't mean to interrupt."

"I welcome your interruption. Maybe we could schedule it in fact."

Our relationship gave us little basis for much small talk so she quickly made her point.

"As far as I know Caliche Hills has never had a murder case before. But that doesn't mean we at the sheriff's office can't handle the investigation."

"I'm sure you can, Aleta." Fortunately, we had enough conversations under our belts that we used first names. Usually that happens within five minutes in the Hill Country.

"Even though the FBI investigates hate crimes, we're still part of the investigation and we get regular updates from any other police agency interested in the case."

I was surprised. "The FBI has investigated George's death?"

"Yes, and they have talked with the San Antonio police quite a bit. There may be a connection with a similar crime in the area. Is there something wrong, Connie?"

"I called the FBI and couldn't get anyone to talk to me."

"Who did you talk to?"

"I'm not sure. Whoever answered the phone."

"What did you tell them?"

"My son was killed as part of a conspiracy."

"A conspiracy?"

"Well, I was speculating."

274

"Have you called other agencies about this?"

"Uhm, no. That is not police-type offices."

"Uh-huh. Connie, could I ask you to do something for me?"

"Of course."

"I really want to bring George's killers to justice. What if you just turned this whole investigation over to me? Could you trust me with that? I know that may be a lot to ask, but I want to do this for you. Would you let me worry about the FBI and conspiracy and whatever else is bothering you about the investigation?"

The afternoon light shone from her face a glowing honey tone, a honeyed angel. That's Aleta Diaz. A five foot three, one hundred fifteen pound honey-toned angel. She could have the whole investigation. I gave her a big hug and sent her on her way to solve the great crime of Caliche Hills. It was her problem now.

I would just go over her head and prod someone in Washington about the conspiracy part and maybe find a better choice than Smitty to be her husband.

# Chapter 45: Composing a Letter

Connie did not know yet who should receive her letter, someone in the Pentagon of course, but she just assumed she could figure that part after writing the letter. The opening line (How dare you rob us of our son without even telling us he had signed up for covert missions!) would force him to read the whole letter. Connie managed three pages about the unfair way government imposes itself upon its citizens and democracy means something about of/by/and for the people. Then she simply quit. She had reached a dead end. She could not come to a final purpose for the letter. What did Connie want this general or under-secretary or whomever to do? So she put the letter in the drawer of her neat little secretary's desk in her bedroom. She did not forget about it. No, indeed, the letter occupied her thoughts constantly.

Connie mentioned it to Francisca Dominguez at church. She did not tell her exactly what was in the letter. Just that she was composing a letter to the officials in D.C. about how shabbily she felt they had been treated because of George's death. Francisca said it sounded like a brilliant idea. The two women never had a chance to discuss just how brilliant it was because Francisca excused herself to run help someone in the kitchen. Connie thought about the fact that her friend had never shown much interest in the work of the fellowship committee the whole time Connie served on that committee, so it appeared she must have developed a new interest no one else knew was there.

## Annie

I fell on my bed and started to cry. Mom is going off the deep end. I need her. When Mama Teresa was sick and died, I worked hard keeping Mom on track. I took care of her. The boys ran circles in their own little world. They had no idea their grandmother was dying and their mother suffered. Grief hurts - a lot. Dad knew, but he's been hip-deep in alligators at work for, I dunno, a long time. None of the three of them knows anything about taking care of Mom. And that means they know nothing about my heartache. I meant to say two of them. But if

George were alive what good would he be. I mashed a pillow into my face so Mom couldn't hear me cry.

The light in the bathroom hurt my eyes but after I washed my face, I felt better. The girl in the mirror wore dark circles under her eyes just above a runny nose and a sad mouth. I scrubbed my face again. She told me I was a selfish brat. Mom, Dad and Stephen missed George as much as I did. Gwennie and Elspeth and Sylvia and Sonita supported me. They cared about my loss. A walk around the back yard felt good. Yeah, it was hot but there was a breeze. Mocking birds were gossiping about the squirrels. A book group of deer - does and yearlings - grazed along the tree line. I figured that meant I could go on with life too. Back inside I told Mom we needed to play a duet. "Yes," she said. "It's time for your lesson." Now that was spooky, but anyway we played for nearly an hour.

Later I thought about her comment. Mom had not been my piano teacher for at least two years so that's why she startled me. But why not? That could be a new avenue for working through our grief. Lord knows I could use the lessons. Or, maybe not, because Mom and I both knew I had gotten past anything she could teach me about the piano. Only that's not what I'm about here. This is all about focusing her attention on me and away from her loss of George. So I went with it.

She is so funny. At first it's all, "Oh, honey, I don't know. What could I teach you?" Yet, before you have to answer that, she's already making with the suggestions. "You know you have gotten a little lazy with your hand position." So now, I'm taking piano lessons. We sit down for an hour every Monday morning. And that means I am practicing every day. I get by with thirty minutes because Mom isn't home either when I practice or she doesn't watch the clock like when I was younger. The surprise to me is that she really does still know more about playing the piano than I do. This was supposed to be my gift to her to pull her out of her distraught mother mode. Turns out, I'm back into learning how to do something I love doing. Neat, huh?

# Chapter 46: Finding the Address

Stephen logged onto the Internet and searched for someone to write at the Pentagon. He gave his mother an address for one of the Undersecretaries of Defense. This one had something to do with personnel and logistics. It sounded like what she wanted.

"What was it like?" She meant the Pentagon on the Internet.

"Propaganda."

"What did you say?" His mother did not approve of his tone.

"Oh, you can find whatever you need to know. But you have to wade through a lot of military/governmental hype to get there."

"Stephen, positive stories about the young people who give up a part of their youth to serve our country is not propaganda."

"Whatever."

"I've heard that word often enough."

Stephen rolled his eyes.

In spite of that attitude, Stephen had helped. She now had an address. Using crisp linen art store stationary she copied her letter - now four pages in longhand. What a relief! This had to be the proper recourse to focus attention on terrorism within our borders. Someone had to listen to her.

## Stephen

George, Dan, and I sometimes did these Internet sessions where we would string together two or three phrases and see what we could come up with on Google. We would see who could come up with the weirdest finds or the least responses. Usually when I use an Internet search engine I get thousands, anyway hundreds of choices. But if I really put together two words that don't ordinarily go together I might get only a half dozen responses. The ultimate win would be to have Google come back with only one selection. Of course, it wasn't hard to put together stuff so ridiculous there was "no match." That didn't count. On the weird side, we found lots of pornography. Once or twice was exciting for hormone rich teen boys. Five or six times was boring. A dozen was disgusting and finally it just got irritating. One time I wanted to follow a link to a chat room. Dan laughed and George said, "No way."

"Why not? It might be fun. We could meet someone new."

"Meet some pervert," said Dan.

"You might find a girlfriend, Stephen," George said. "Then someday discover she's a forty-year-old hit-man in the federal penitentiary."

"There's no telling who you're gonna run into," said Dan.

No way to know who might be out there.

## Chapter 47: Arrests

Smitty and Aleta came by to report that two boys had confessed to beating George, and two others have also been arrested. Would they go to jail was all Connie asked. Smitty wanted to tell her who they were and where they lived but Aleta cut him off. She turned him around and pushed him out the door in mid-sentence. "We're done here," she told him.

She is such a good girl, caring and all, Connie thought. That foolish young man better open his eyes before she found someone more promising.

Arthur already knew about it when he got home. He spoke of how relieved he was they had been caught but said they don't need to go to the trial or ever see them. "Don't you want to know why they killed George?" Connie asked him. He said they did not know themselves, how were they going to explain anything to us. Later they learned all four boys had confessed and a date was set for an arraignment hearing. Arthur changed

his mind at that point and said they could
attend the hearing.

## Annie

Stephen warned me to keep my eyes
covered while I counted. I always did even
though I knew he peeked. "One, two, three,"
I started. At twenty, I was counting by fives.
At fifty, I changed to tens. "One hundred!"
All the world should know I was coming
looking for my brothers. George who thinks
he is so smart hides behind those low bushes
with the small red flowers. I know where he
is, he runs faster than either of us so why
bother. Stephen disappears like a ninja turtle.
I don't so much try to find him as I simply
outrun him once he springs from his hole.
It's not so hot in the shade. We're nine to
twelve years old and wearing shorts, tee
shirts and sneakers. The humidity runs down
my sides and all over my face. A white flash
on the left. I spin and dart toward base but a
cedar root snags my foot, the ground slaps
the wind from my tummy, dirt and twigs fill
my mouth. I can't breathe or yell. My
twisted ankle throbs. I'm alone and I hear
nothing from either brother. I push myself

into a sitting position. A searing pain in my gut releases a howl. My sobs announce that I can breathe again. George kneels next to me; Stephen looks down.

"Where did you go? I'm hurt!"

"We're right here. We came to find you."

"I hurt my ankle - all by myself."

"Not as long as you have two brothers. You're not all by yourself."

## Chapter 48: Arraignment

Arthur stepped into the courtroom and then moved aside for Connie, Annie, and Stephen to precede him. He pointed to the back row where they seated themselves. An air of professional busyness permeated the room. Someone had told them a courtroom sometimes divides very much like a wedding, family and friends of the offended on one side behind the prosecuting attorneys, family and friends of the offender on the other behind the defense table. Sylvester, Marie, and Dan followed the Thompsons and sat with them. Lance and Willow came in a few minutes later and sat immediately in front of them. The men nodded to one another, the women exchanged a few words. All three families adopted the behavior they would choose if visiting an unfamiliar high liturgy church. The adults stared straight ahead or down at their laps. Dan and Stephen slumped over, elbows on knees. Annie looked around quickly and then thumb-pressed a pleat into her skirt. Before long, attorneys and uniformed officers filled the fenced off area before the judge's bench. A side door opened and more uniformed officers brought in four young men in orange prison jump suits. The common distinguishing feature of the four was their color. All blood had drained from each of their faces. The first three shuffled to their assigned seats head down. The last searched across the courtroom with fear-enlarged eyes before he, too, found his seat. A muffled sob accompanied their sitting.

Connie looked toward the rows immediately behind the defense table. A woman reached forward and touched one of the boys. She looked fortyish, small, and dark. What could be seen of shoulders showed a shiny navy short-sleeved blouse. On her far side sat a fat sullen man whose dark suit coat was tight on his shoulders. Sitting on the near side of the couple was a woman who might just be the first mother's sister. A glance at the two of them raised the question of whether she was here because of her nephew, or could two of the boys be cousins? The man beside the apparent sister wore a pressed western style white shirt. He looked several years older. His ears stuck out under thinning grey hair. Beside and behind them several others hunched over as though heavy weights pulled their foreheads toward the seat backs before them.

Everyone stood as a judge entered, an imposing man in a black robe who may be Hispanic. Someone recited the reason these youths were before the court. One of the prosecuting attorneys stood and commented in something of a nasal twang on the charges. The judge asked for a response from the defense. A short woman with black curls around her face stood to tell the judge she spoke for the attorneys representing the young men. She explained that all four had admitted their guilt but there were mitigating circumstances.

"You're going to argue drunkenness as a mitigating circumstance." The judge was not asking a question.

"Yes, your honor."

The judge scowled over his reading glasses.

"Here's what we're going to do," he began. He then set a court date and explained what questions would be decided at that time. After a few questions and comments between the attorneys and the judge, an officer led the four boys from the courtroom.

Arthur stood and motioned for his family to leave. Dan's family moved into the aisle allowing Annie, Stephen, and Dan to head for the door. Connie shifted slowly toward Marie the whole time watching the gathering behind the defense table. Taking their cue from Connie, the other adults turned in that direction also. The woman who first got her attention by her cry remained seated. Two women stood and were held by men. A low murmuring of questions and tears rumbled across the room.

"We should go," whispered Arthur. They left.

Outside the courtroom, Lance asked Arthur if he planned to return. Arthur grimaced. He told Lance he could not see the point of returning.

"Uh-huh." Lance nodded his head. "Moving forward, right?"

"Exactly."

"Thank you."

Arthur stopped, gave Lance a puzzled look.

Lance smiled. "You're my role model, Arthur. I'm learning a lot by watching you." He turned away with Willow and then turned back. "By the way, Art, I contacted one of those ministers I told you about."

Arthur frowned, trying to remember what minister this might be.

Lance stepped back toward him. "I am going help raise signatures on a petition to ask the Presbyterian General Assembly to recognize the ordination of gays."

Connie herded Annie and Stephen past Arthur and toward their car. "What was that about, Art?"

He shook his head. "I think the lake is turning over."

## Arthur

I did not know any of them. Not the parents, not the boys, not the people with them. I had never seen any of those people before in my life. Our local newspaper frequently uses a filler statement that says, "Strangers are merely friends we have yet to meet." Or killers? But these people weren't ... But, yes, they were. The boys were.

## Chapter 49: The Extent of Loss

Connie asked Marie what she thought.

"I don't know what to think," is how she started out but later she said, "Maybe it's best. Maybe Art is right. You know those boys, whoever they are brought tragedy to your family. Now they are learning that they have imposed tragedy on their own families."

Connie had not even thought about that. Four families are now devastated because of their rashness. So she made quite a speech about it.

"Marie," she said, "surely no one would purposefully plot to kill a young man and then spend the rest of their life in prison or maybe be executed. Nobody would intentionally crush their mother and daddy with the pain of that loss, the loss of being removed from a loved child for the remainder of their earthly existence. It had to be a rash action. They were drunk or stoned or - I just don't know what. But it had to be some spur-of-the moment stupidity."

Marie took Connie's hands and looked at her for the longest time. A hint of a smile flirted with the corners of her mouth.

"You are absolutely correct," she said. "Do you understand what you have just said?"

"Of course I do. I'm not drunk or stoned or acting rashly."

"No, honey, you are about as clear-headed as I have seen you all summer."


## Annie

My job is vacuuming. I like it. The first part goes fast because Penny plays with the vacuum. Then she gets tired so I change the game. I vacuum by design. I'll go in squares and diamonds, circles and half arcs. As long as I have been aware of vacuum cleaners, we have used canisters with the tubey things. Somehow, a nest of wasps got into the laundry room. Penny decided to nap in there after she had finished her share of the vacuuming. I heard her yelp and then race by me. When I saw the wasp, I did the most natural thing someone could do with a vacuum in my hands. I sucked up every one of those wasps into the cleaner. Then I thought what am I going to do when I turn this thing off? Wasp spray! I knew we had some. In fact, it was supposed to be right here in the laundry room. But I couldn't find any there. I looked in the hall closet, not because I expected to find a can of wasp spray there but because it was the next storage-closet place to look for things. Sure enough, no wasp spray, but there was a box on the shelf that looked out of place but somehow familiar. The card on it was addressed to Seaman Thompson in Elspeth's handwriting. Uh-oh, I thought, what are we going to do with this? I shoved it back on the shelf. This would have to wait.

# Chapter 50: Writing a Script

The Thompsons all became adept at telling people they would keep their distance from any legal proceedings. Caliche Hills popularized a new conversational gambit: "Would you attend the trial if you were a Thompson?" Almost universally, people answered "Yes!" Of course, the intensity increased as people provided explanations. Predictably neighbors and friends chose either "To see justice done" or "To find closure" for their answer.

Arthur called a family council so they could write their own script. The skeleton came from the father but both Annie and Stephen contributed salient points.

First talking point: We will not follow the trial process. Why? Because our loss of son/brother George pains us deeply. We grieve over George. That is enough burden to carry right now.

Second talking point: The four families of the boys on trial face their own tragedies and do not need the added weight of our presence.

Third talking point: We cannot sit at the judge's table, behind either the prosecution or defense table or in the jury. Justice will be done without us.

Fourth talking point: We are moving ahead in our own lives just fine, thank you very much.

Connie took private pride in the fact that she did not contribute anything to the script, at least that she can remember. In fact, she was not initially sure she understood it. Arthur frowned as he talked, punctuating his points by stabbing his finger on the coffee table. Stephen would answer, "Yeah, yeah, and I think ..." Annie would offer her usual, "What if we, like, you know ..."

Connie felt good watching them process the script. She did not have to understand. The one feeling she did remember was disagreement. She had no interest in going to the San Antonio courthouse to gawk at a murder trial. However, the reasons her family manufactured answered nothing for her. The important point was the family council. The family produced the script. The family adopted it unanimously. She liked that. So, Connie memorized everything her husband and children wrote. Annie typed it on her laptop and printed four copies.

The next day Connie called Marie and read it to her. Later she called Francisca Dominguez and read it to her. One afternoon she went to her art store and recited it to the kids working the shop. On the way home, she told several people at the grocery store how "we Thompsons" felt about the upcoming trial. By then she was embellishing it some. At week's end, she owned it.

## Connie

I looked at Marie and said flatly, "I will never get over this."

Marie was helping me clean out my "dumping spot." I use an old laundry basket that I keep in a cabinet in the laundry room for dumping. In it, I usually find recipes needing to be filed, articles someone wants me to read, advertising circulars for items I haven't finally decided not to buy and plain junk that I need two stages before throwing away. For some reason Marie felt led to help me sort through the basket and, after a bit, I realized why. I had thrown in my dumping spot copies of George's funeral service, newspaper articles about his beating and death, and all the cards, notes, and letters we had received.

"There are less than ten items here that you will want to save," she told me rather matter-of-factly. "Let's find them and put them in a folder for a future scrapbook and throw away the rest."

I was distressed. "Marie, it's only been a few weeks. I can't discard any of this yet."

She patted my back. "It's been two and a half months, Connie. Annie and Stephen start back to school in two weeks. I know I'm being a little pushy here. But how about you let George rest and give your other kids their mother back?"

Therefore, we sorted. I did not agree to throw anything out from the basket. What she did get from me was an agreement that ten items would be stored respectfully in a drawer in my secretary's desk. Everything else would go in a separate box and return to the laundry room cabinet. That wasn't so hard. Actually seven items set themselves apart from the rest - the funeral service bulletin, an obituary from the mortuary, a card from an aunt, and four different articles from newspapers.

Standing in the great room, she complemented me on my successful decision-making. Then she warned me that we would eventually have to tackle George's room.

"Soon," I said without any conviction.

She turned toward the door and then turned back. "Never is a word only God should use, honey."

After a minute she continued, "There," she smiled, "is our hope."

When she was gone, I sat down on our sofa. Sunbeams danced in the light from the back windows. Outside I could hear the Mueller's spaniel barking at squirrels. Penny lifted her head and gruffed at the noise. I lay my head back and stared at the ceiling. "Never ever, ever never, never ever," I said to the ceiling fan. Maybe the sleeping pills Doc Sauerwein had given me really were helping. I had begun to feel more relaxed the last few days. I reached up to brush hair out of my face and knocked the seven selected items out of my other hand. I picked up the top paper and began to read the story of George's death.

The paper's editor used clear and simple phrases to tell his readers that George Thompson was a fine young man, a recent graduate of Caliche Hills high school. He died because of a savage beating given him by unknown thugs. Five paragraphs all contained on the front page. A tragedy for the family and the community. A tragedy, but no conspiracy, no terrorism. Had he missed something? Or had I?

## Chapter 51: Calling Coach Throckmorton

When Connie called the house, Mrs. Throckmorton told her that Coach was at the school. Connie didn't think anybody went to the school during the summer but Mrs. Throckmorton assured her he spent a lot of time there during the summer. Coach answered Connie's call and invited her to his office.

"This is all new to me," Connie told him.

"I seldom see parents here," he acknowledged.

Mellow earth tones filled his cubbyhole of an office. With no chairs, or no empty ones anyway, they stood for a moment and then he led the mother to the trophy case in the hall where he sought out those George helped win for CHHS. Their steps echoed through the student-less cavern. Coach compared George to previous students. He rattled on a list of statistics, gave her a lecture on what leadership means for a team. The point being that George played an invaluable role in his golf team. She smiled and listened. She really did not care about most of what he told her except it sounded good for George's memory. Finally, he ran down enough that she could ask him a couple of questions. He seemed pleasantly surprised and gave her the information she sought. It was a good day.

## Connie

"Arthur," I wanted to know. "What does IMHO mean?"

"Where did you hear that?" He asked me over the top of his book.

"Stephen and Annie both use it."

"Oh, sure, they would. That's email shorthand for 'in my humble opinion.'"

"It's not teen-age slang or something?"

"No, not necessarily. I suppose teens are more likely to use it."

He put down his book and frowned. Picking up the book again he said, "No, everybody who emails me uses that and BTW - by the way. You know, it's like ASAP."

"Well, that's good. I can use that."

"Use what? IMHO? How?"

"All right. Here it is. IMHO we need to establish a golf scholarship in George's name."

At this point, I put down my book and looked at Art. "George was a good boy. He was a hero of a son. I think we need to establish a golf scholarship in his name at Texas State."

He looked at me with such a pained, loving look. "Okay. Yeah, okay. We can do that."

He stood and pulled me to him smothering me in his hug.

# Chapter 52: The A. D.'s Office

From any direction travelers approach San Marcos Texas, they can't miss the red roofed building on the top of the highest hill in town. Old Main, the first building at Texas State University marks the campus. Most Hill Country residents have not gotten accustomed to the name Texas State since they have always known it as Southwest Texas, or Southwest Texas State Teachers College when LBJ attended. Strahan Coliseum sits on the edge of the campus, housing a basketball arena a visitor would guess. Connie did not know what else. She and Arthur were looking for and found the Athletic Director's office.

A handsome man, who probably had been an athlete in some sport or other, the Athletic Director showed the Thompsons into a room much larger and nicer than Coach Throckmorton's cramped quarters at CHHS.

After settling comfortably he looked first at Mr. Thompson and then at Mrs. Thompson.

"Our son George," she started.

"George Thompson was your son?" His eyebrows pressed upward against his hairline.

She nodded.

"I watched your son play a tournament here on our course. Very fine young man. I talked to him about playing golf at TSU. We had our hopes up. I am so sorry for your loss Mrs. Thompson and Mr. Thompson."

Connie knew they were doing the right thing.

## Connie

The next day I called Elspeth. "Elspeth, honey, could you come over for supper tomorrow night?" She hesitated a moment and then quickly agreed she could come.

"¿Que pasa?" she wanted to know.

"Well," I answered, "I found a box in my hall closet. You brought a present for Seaman Thompson. I'd like for you to tell us about it and maybe we might all tell George stories for one evening."

I'm so glad she said she would come. Now I need to tell Art, Annie, and Stephen. Maybe

I will invite Dan and his parents. We'll have tacos and enchiladas.

## Acknowledgments

Many friends and family have offered
advice and encouragement. I particularly
appreciate the helpful comments from Betsy
Gruelich. I am better because Maralee
knows how I am made.

## About the author

Jerry M. Self is a native of Wichita, Kansas.
He has settled for a time in Texas and
Tennessee and now lives with his wife
Maralee in Albuquerque, New Mexico.

# Also by Jerry M. Self

*Who Says How She Died?*

Lance and Willow Carroll agonize through the illness and death of Zinnia Foster, an advocate for pregnant teens in Albuquerque, New Mexico. Her life focused on the moral issues surrounding pregnancy. Her death raised a new set of issues concerning the right to decide how one leaves this life.

## Praise for Who Says How She Died?

A wonderful look at the many dilemmas we face regarding health, day to day living challenges & end of life issues. The perspectives provided are thought provoking and should be useful to all, regardless of their age and status in life. I highly recommend this book! – *A Central Texas reader*

Eager for next page: Realistic head on approach to current life and death issues.

Great book for small group discussion. – *A Tennessee perspective*

True to life situations with likable characters. You are drawn into the lives of the characters as they help their friends deal with their struggles. Lots of food for thought. Loved Miss Zinnia. Looking forward to Jerry Self's next book. – *A reader from Oklahoma*

Very thought provoking, relevant story line. Would be a great book for discussion groups, book clubs, small groups. Deals with the ethics in the health care industry and dying with dignity. – *A New Mexican*

Fast paced and grapples with some sensitive social dilemmas. – *An East Texan*

## The Who3 Series

The *Who3 Series* uses throw-away phrases – Who says? Who knows? Who cares? – to raise serious questions: where do we find a viable source of authority, accurate

information, or meaningful compassion?
Watch for the third volume, *Who Cares?* –
coming soon.